CW00421761

The Sound of Murder

Retired from the Sussex police and on holiday in Salzburg to visit his old friend Inspector Leo Kiesler, Ralph Brand found himself staying at the same hotel as the film crew for *The Sound of Murder*. The low-budget film was trading deliberately on *The Sound of Music* and was designed to give a starring role to Matthew Armstrong, best known for his portrayal of a police inspector in a popular TV series. Brand had already met Armstrong briefly. Now he met Ella, Armstrong's Austrian wife, the aging Austrian actress Lotte Bruckner, and other members of the crew.

It was obvious that there were tensions among them; that Armstrong had something to hide; that the production company was only waiting for a chance to pull out of the whole operation. But none of this explained why Ella Armstrong confided to Brand that she went in fear of her life.

Soon the hotel was alive with the sound of murder, and Brand, far from being retired, found himself assisting Leo Kiesler in what proved one of the most complex cases of his career.

MARGARET HINXMAN

The Sound of
Murder

COLLINS, 8 GRAFTON STREET, LONDON W1

William Collins Sons & Co. Ltd
London · Glasgow · Sydney · Auckland
Toronto · Johannesburg

First published 1986
© Margaret Hinxman 1986

British Library Cataloguing in Publication Data

Hinxman, Margaret
  The sound of murder.—(Crime Club)
  I. Title
  823'.914[F]   PR6058.I537

  ISBN 0-00-232081-9

Photoset in Linotron Baskerville by
Rowland Phototypesetting Ltd
Bury St Edmunds, Suffolk
Printed in Great Britain by
William Collins Sons & Co. Ltd, Glasgow

CHAPTER 1

'You're late!'

The girl squinted accusingly at the baggy-tweeded man in his late sixties. She had the harassed air of someone who had her mind on six aggravations already and could barely support another.

The man turned towards her, amusement and surprise fighting for possession of his weathered features. 'I'm sorry?' The nuance of a question rather than an apology escaped her.

'I suppose the plane was delayed. It's always that—or something else.' Her expression softened and fleetingly composed itself into a smile. Quite a nice, dimpled smile. But it vanished as quickly as it had surfaced.

'Someone really should have met you. But after Arthur's heart attack you can imagine it's been pretty chaotic. What with everything—and that damned woman.' She pulled herself up sharply, apparently regretting the reference to that 'damned woman'. 'We were lucky to get you at such short notice. Your agent said you were free for a week. It's only a couple of scenes, as you know. A spit and a cough, but vital. And we've rearranged the schedule to fit them in. I'm afraid you won't have time to unpack. I've got a car laid on. The producer, Jake, is on the location and he wants to see you right away. Oh yes, here's a copy of the script. You can read it on the way. But I shouldn't pay too much attention to it. Your scenes have been rewritten. They're the green pages. By the way, my name's Debbie Price, production coordinator.' The grand-sounding title, lately elevated from the more prosaic production secretary, instantly conferred on her a status that demanded respect. She was, too, older than she had first appeared to be.

She thrust a bulky, photocopied manuscript, bound in cardboard, into the man's hands.

He stared bemused at the legend on the cover, *The Sound of Murder*, then looked up at the girl.

'I think there's some mistake.'

She squinted more piercingly at him. 'Mistake! You *are* Jeremy Fox. The actor.'

'Afraid not. Ralph Brand.'

'I'm Fox.' A meek, breathless voice floated across the lobby from the entrance to the hotel. 'Sorry I'm late . . . the plane . . .' The voice petered out as the girl moved closer to them, inspecting first one man then the other beadily. They were roughly the same build, age and similar in type.

'Oh Lord, another balls-up. My fault,' she said, including both men in her apology. 'I lost a contact lens in the washbasin this morning and I left my spare specs upstairs.'

She grabbed the script from Brand's hand and deposited it with the rightful owner, now looking as puzzled as Brand, whom she dismissed with another of her brisk, brief smiles. As she ushered the bewildered actor, lamely questioning the security of his luggage, towards the waiting car, Brand heard her repeating the same recital of woes. 'Someone really should have met you. But after Arthur's heart attack . . .'

Brand chuckled and turned to the reception desk where the head porter, who had witnessed the odd little scene of mistaken identity, shrugged his shoulders and lifted his hands in mock supplication.

'Film units! I'm so sorry, Herr Brand. When Inspector Kiesler booked your room we didn't know they'd be here. But they won't interfere with your comfort. It's just the production office and staff and some of the artists. The crew are in the bigger hotels in the city. The Mariahof doesn't cater for those numbers.' Or, his tone indicated, those people. His English was courtly and correct, yet unmistakably alien, in the manner of head porters all over the world.

'You seem to know a lot about film units,' Brand said as

he signed the registry form and offered his passport.

'Well, we did play host to *The Sound of Music*,' the man replied quaintly.

'Biggest thing that happened to Salzburg since Mozart, eh?!'

The head porter covered his mouth with his white-gloved hand, not quite suppressing a rogue smile. Brand warmed to him, suspecting that they were much of an age and had seen too much of life to be thrown by irritations of the moment.

'I think you'll like your room. It's overlooking the city and there's a small balcony. If there's anything you need don't hesitate to call on me.'

'That's most kind of you, Herr . . .?'

The man looked surprised. Not many guests bothered with the names of the hotel staff. Those who provided service were usually anonymous robots who only acquired an identity when something went wrong. He didn't know Brand, who liked to put a name to a face, perhaps because most of his working life had been spent trying to match the two.

'Sommer. Fritz Sommer,' the man said grudgingly, as if it went against the grain to be on such personal terms with guests. He rang a bell smartly and a uniformed youth emerged seemingly from nowhere.

'*Vier-und-zwanzig*,' he said curtly, indicating Brand's two suitcases and handing him the metal key marked 24.

As Brand followed the pageboy along the corridor, a mild altercation appeared to be taking place behind the open door of *Ein-und-zwanzig* which bore a discreet notice, as befitted the Mariahof: '*The Sound of Murder: Production Office*.' Amid the muffled anger a raised voice exploded. 'That damned woman!' The voice wasn't Debbie Price's. Whoever the damned woman was, thought Brand, she wasn't choosey about whom she offended.

Professionally he was intrigued. But personally he couldn't care less. Ralph Brand was luxuriating in the first real holiday he'd had in years, even though his former colleagues in the Sussex constabulary jokingly insisted that retirement was one perpetual holiday.

'I'm going to enjoy myself,' he murmured, grunting with pleasure as he leaned over the tiny balcony, surveying the city of Salzburg beneath him. In the distance he could see the fortress of Hohensalzburg towering protectively, like a benign guardian, over the maze of bustling shopping lanes, arcades and gardens. The Salzach river threaded its way lazily between the old city and the new. Maybe, like the Danube, it wasn't really blue. But the eye of the beholder on the balcony convinced itself that it was.

He sniffed the air appreciatively. Even the promise of rain didn't cloud his pleasure. In a few weeks there wouldn't be a room to spare as the summer festival drew music-lovers from all over the world. But even now in the late spring the city vibrated to the music of Strauss and Lehár and Schubert in anticipation of the greater celebration of Mozart in the months to come. Little pockets of schoolchildren in dirndls and lederhosen would suddenly surface in the Domplatz and the Mirabell gardens singing for the sheer joy of it under the meticulous eyes and beat of their choirmasters.

His old friend, Inspector Leo Kiesler of the Salzburg City police, had chosen well, both the time and the hotel, thought Brand. The city wasn't yet so crowded that you couldn't move around freely and the Mariahof was large enough to accommodate all the amenities yet sufficiently personal to extend to its guests a feeling of well-being which all the guide books had told Brand was characteristically Austrian.

He felt strangely light-headed, glad that he'd finally acted on Leo's urging to visit Salzburg now that he was retired. Theirs had been an intermittent friendship, largely conducted by telephone and correspondence in Brand's halting German and Kiesler's shamingly fluent English. They'd met some years before when Brand was still a detective-inspector on the force in Sussex. An Austrian national had been involved in drug-smuggling and Brand had gone out of his way to be helpful to the Inspector from Salzburg who had been sent over to cooperate with the British police. They had established an instant rapport and liking, although the Austrian was twenty years younger than Brand.

He poured himself a cup of the coffee he'd ordered and set about making his sightseeing plans for the afternoon. But as he plotted his exploratory route memories of that odd encounter in the lobby that morning kept intruding. He wondered how the flustered Jeremy Fox was getting on, whether his 'spit and a cough' was worth the trip, whether that 'damned woman' was throwing her weight about. And who the hell was she? However much he told himself that it was none of his business, that he wasn't on duty, hadn't been for four years now, the habits of a lifetime died hard.

He tried to shake the speculations that were racing through his mind, to persuade himself that he was here as a tourist, not as a detective. He'd returned to the business of mapping a walk through to the inner city and maybe taking in a visit to the Mozart museum when the telephone by his bedside rang.

It was Kiesler.

'My good friend, at last, you're here,' said the welcoming voice. 'You're settled. Is the room all right? You like the Mariahof? It's my favourite. Need you wonder why? The family is anxious to see you. They've heard so much about you. Tonight? You've no plans? I'll pick you up at eight. Maria is preparing a special dinner.'

Brand assured him that everything was perfect, it would be his great pleasure to meet the family that night. But it was difficult to get a word in edgewise. He recognized the abstracted tone of a busy man stealing a few minutes from Lord knows how many demands on his time to be polite to a friend. He attempted to wrap up the telephone call quickly. Tonight they'd have time.

He heard Kiesler rap out an answer to an underling's

question in German. 'Sorry, Ralph. It's these movie people. Crazy people! They want to block off the Mirabell to tourists for the day. Of course they can't. I'm afraid you have some of them staying at the Mariahof. I can't apologize enough.'

'No apologies needed. You forget. I'm a cinema buff.' Later he'd tell Kiesler about his brush with them that morning and they'd laugh. But not now.

'I can't tell you the trouble we have with them. I'm surprised the city fathers allowed them to shoot here—after the last time. I think they were swayed by the producer. Schneider. His father was Austrian. The tradesmen say they bring money. Salzburg has a festival, scenery, visitors. *That's* money. Well, we'll get them out by high season. And good riddance. I must go, Ralph. You understand. Tonight at eight.'

Brand smiled as he replaced the receiver. He understood. How he understood! He hadn't had to cope with many film crews in his part of Sussex. But he knew the problems: traffic control, clearing streets, placating irate locals, not that there had been many of those. Most people were fascinated by the process of film-making and the proximity of stars. Ah well, that was Kiesler's problem, not his.

He spent a pleasant afternoon exploring that part of the city within walking distance, promising himself a visit to Hellbrunn Palace with its trick fountains, to the Marionette Theatre and a sightseeing excursion to *The Sound of Music* locations, the latter, he admitted to himself, a childish treat. But really, why not? He would be just one of the thousands of tourists who crowded the coaches that daily plied the route where Julie Andrews erupted into song on the top of a mountain and met Christopher Plummer at the majestic Leopoldskron castle—which was a lot grander than the actual home of the Trapp family portrayed in the film.

When he returned to the hotel, looking forward to a good dinner that evening (a sausage and a roll had sufficed to ward off the pangs of hunger), the lobby was in a turmoil.

The threatening weather had curtailed shooting on *The Sound of Murder*. Debbie Price wearing spectacles—presumably she hadn't managed to locate the elusive contact lens—was discussing 'call sheets' with a ferrety-looking young man in blue jeans and anorak. Another man festooned with cameras was grumbling to nobody in particular that he couldn't be expected to take good still photographs when the director didn't even care. Supposedly the director was out of earshot. A group of what Brand took to be actors, Jeremy Fox among them, made damply for the bar. A pretty young woman with a businesslike manner was firmly assuring two worried companions that with luck 'you'll get both Matthew and Judy Clay tomorrow, but they refuse to be interviewed in the evening.'

Someone mentioned 'rushes' and the ferrety young man groaned. A tall, corpulent man with a bald head and an unfortunate cast in one eye, which gave the impression that he was looking in two directions at once, was making some annoying demand of the head porter who nodded placatingly while seemingly not budging an inch.

Then, above the general hubbub, a piercing voice threw everyone into a state of hush.

'You, Mr Schneider' the voice commanded.

The corpulent man with the cast in his eye froze for an instant, then turned round with a beatific smile on his face that had been put on in the instant of turning.

'Ella!'

The woman smiled back icily. The smile lifted the corners of her mouth but didn't reach her eyes.

'We still have that little problem to discuss, Jake.'

'Ella, my dear.' He kissed the cheek that was obviously anything but dear. She submitted perfunctorily, then removed her cheek as if she feared contamination.

'You promised. A suite at least or an apartment. Do you realize we're on the same floor as the production office? What kind of treatment is that for your star? My husband is used to having the best.' Brand's keen ear caught the trace of an accent, all but buried in her command of English. But it was there.

'The best? On a British Television series?' His mocking tone implied that the best on a Television series was distinctly below par.

The woman eyed him coldly. 'Don't be facetious. He was accorded a proper respect for his status.'

'I'm not being facetious, Ella,' he lied. 'But you must appreciate that we had to take the accommodation we could get here. Salzburg is a big tourist centre.'

'Tourists!' she sniffed.

'Ella, please, let's talk about it later.' The new voice sounded familiar to Brand, but he couldn't quite place it.

A man in a crumpled raincoat, which looked as if it might be a wardrobe prop to establish a character, extricated himself from the group of actors hot-footing it for the bar. With his back to Brand, he put his arm around the angry Ella. He did it so solicitiously that Brand half expected to hear him say, 'There, there, never mind.'

'Well, all right,' she said grudgingly. 'But you're too easy.'

The assembled company, which seemed to have been holding its breath in suspense, started talking among itself again as if nothing had happened.

Debbie Price lifted an eyebrow in recognition of Brand. 'Sorry about this morning. Must dash. Catch you later. Call sheets for tomorrow,' she said hurriedly, assuming, as all closely knit film units do, that only a fool wouldn't know what a call sheet was—the schedule, location and cast required for the next day's shooting.

As the company drifted off, Brand studied the revolving stand of postcards. Like most tourists, he'd sworn he wouldn't send any and then couldn't wait to alert his friends back home that he was where he was.

Admiring a particularly striking view of the Tyrol, he felt a tap on his shoulder.

The voice that had lately been placating the difficult Ella said warmly, 'Don't I know you?' Good God, not another clone of me, thought Brand. Or surely he couldn't be mistaken for Jeremy Fox yet again that day!

CHAPTER 2

'It's Brand, isn't it? Inspector Brand. Matthew Armstrong.'

The face Brand turned to greet was as familiar to him as his own. The surprise was that Matthew Armstrong should remember him.

Caught off guard, he could think only of a lame response. 'How could I forget? I've been watching you on Television practically every week for the last five years.'

'I don't mean that, old boy.' Only Matthew Armstrong could brush aside his own celebrity so casually, probably because he'd never believed it. 'I mean Worthing. The Connaught theatre. How many years ago?! Just before I got the *Braddock* series. I always meant to write and tell you what a big help you were to me. But I never got around to it. You know how it is.'

It was flattering to be recognized, but Brand still couldn't fathom why he'd made such an impression on Armstrong, who must have met hundreds of people since then, although he himself remembered the actor very well. It had been only a simple case of theft from the actor's hotel room when he'd been playing a two-week season at the Connaught in a fairly inferior production of a very inferior thriller. The inept thief had been an employee at the hotel who'd made the silly mistake of trying to flog Armstrong's gold watch, cuff-links and tiepin to a local jeweller.

'Just in the line of duty. It was hardly in the Great Train Robbery league.' He recalled they'd met socially several times during Armstrong's stay in the Sussex town over pints in a pub, discussing their shared interest in show business. But after that their paths hadn't crossed.

Armstrong threw back his handsome head and laughed. 'You still don't get it, old boy.' The 'old boy' bit was beginning to irritate Brand. It hit too close to home, although Armstrong didn't mean it that way. 'I modelled Braddock, the character, on you. Well, bits and pieces. Good, solid detective-inspector who didn't get promotion because he didn't play by the rule book.'

Brand wasn't sure how good and solid a detective-inspector he'd been. But he certainly hadn't rated promotion and, as his former sergeant, John Waller, could testify, he hadn't played by the rule book. It wasn't much of a recommendation for all his years on the Force.

'To tell you the truth, I can't say I noticed.' The series had been tough, tricky and glossy and any resemblance to the hard, patient slog of real life police detection had seemed purely coincidental.

'Well, I suppose you wouldn't,' Armstrong conceded. 'You know what these TV tyros are like. Keep it entertaining, plenty of action and wrap up all the loose ends in fifty minutes. But you were there, I promise you. Very calm, laid back.'

Brand smiled. He wondered if Matthew Armstrong had any idea of the turmoil of confusion behind that calm, laid-back manner.

'Of course it was the sheerest luck getting to know you when I was up for the series. I got a chance to observe how a detective actually works. Gave me an edge when it came to choosing between me and the other fellers. I could give them a characterization, a point of view, straight off. When they bring in the police consultants during the production you can't get close to them. It's all—just show business.'

Brand hadn't realized they'd got that close all those years before, but he did recall they'd had some very enlightening chats. More enlightening to Brand than to Armstrong, he'd thought. Like most actors, Armstrong was obsessively concerned about himself, his career and the fear of failure, to the exclusion of almost everything else. At the time, reduced to heading the cast in a provincial production that played to half full houses at night and a handful of pensioners at matinees, failure for Matthew Armstrong had seemed a distinct possibility. *Braddock* had changed all that. Late in his career, the public had discovered in Armstrong an heroic figure. He had found his niche as a world-weary heart-throb, with muscles and fan mail to prove it. With the possible exception of his agent, no one was more surprised than Matthew.

'I say, old chap, what about a drink? Early night. Rain stopped play. I gather you realize I'm in this epic they're shooting here.'

Brand looked pointedly at his watch. It was six-thirty.

'Oh, come on, just a quick one,' Armstrong urged.

'Matthew!' At the sound of that commanding voice the actor's face sagged into an expression of deep resignation. The change was instant. Before he'd seemed bouncy, sure of himself. Now he looked nervy, anxious.

'You haven't met my wife, Ella, have you, Brand? Why don't we all go for a drink.' It was almost as if he were begging Brand to remain, to give him back some of the confidence that had momentarily drained out of him at the approach of his wife.

Brand nodded. Kiesler wouldn't be calling for him until eight. He had time. But more important, he was intrigued. Armstrong hadn't struck him as the type who would allow himself to be a hen-pecked husband. But he certainly seemed to be giving that impression. Then again he was an actor. Persuading people to believe what he wanted them to believe was his trade.

He let himself be ushered forward to greet the formidable Ella.

'This is Inspector Brand, Ella. Remember I told you

about him? That robbery I had in Worthing.'

She clasped Brand's hand in a cool, firm grip and he found himself looking down into a pair of shrewd, feline eyes which made him feel she were privy to his thoughts. He'd known eyes like that before. Sometimes they'd belonged to saints, sometimes to sinners. He wondered into which category Ella Armstrong fell.

'I remember. He used you in *Braddock*.' She smiled and the eyes seemed to change colour, warmer, more welcoming. 'But not a lot, I think, Inspector Brand.'

'No longer Inspector. Retired. I'm on holiday.'

'You know Salzburg?'

'I know of it. I've a friend in the city police department.'

'Then we're in very good hands.' Armstrong looked sharply at his wife. 'If anything should happen, Matthew. Like another robbery.'

The huddle of actors looked up as they entered the crowded bar, waved cheerily at Matthew, then buried their noses in their drinks with loud cries of '*Prost*' when they saw Ella.

The barman, who had made it his business to sort out the order of precedence in the film unit hierarchy as soon as they'd arrived, beamed, inclined his head and indicated a free table in the corner.

Over a very small schnapps (he was too conscious of having eaten frugally that day), Brand employed his dual talents of appearing to chat amiably while studying the man and woman on either side of him.

At first appearance, Matthew Armstrong hardly seemed to have changed at all since the last time they'd met. But now he began to notice differences. At the Connaught theatre he'd been more careless of his appearance, paunchier in the midriff, thicker around the jawline, approaching middle age and not particularly liking it, but resigned. There'd been that faint air of defeat about him. He'd been a good-looking young leading man who had grown older not too well, still handsome enough behind that footlights, but probably not up to the cruel examination of the camera.

In the intervening years the youth appeared miraculously to have flooded back into him. But it was a manufactured youth, obviously the product of stringent diet, exercise and will. Whether it was his will or Ella's, Brand had yet to find out. His skin wore the slightly sallow, unnatural tan that came from sun lamps rather than sunshine. Yet the result, the image projected through the camera, was impressive. He had to be in his middle fifties, but he'd reached the stage where age seemed immaterial.

As Brand observed him, he noticed that Ella observed too. She was constantly correcting him, cautioning him about the wisdom of a second drink, patting his hand when he made a witticism and caressing the becoming lock of dyed brown hair that fell across his forehead.

Matthew accepted the attention with a good grace honed, thought Brand, over years of experience with his wife's little ways. Most other men would have found her fussing irritating. But he seemed to receive it both as his due and the price he was required to pay. For what? Puzzling!

More puzzling was Ella. Though petite and well groomed, she was no beauty. To Brand she had something more interesting than beauty, the kind of provocative plainness, verging on the ugly, which some sophisticated women manage to transform into a seductive glamour. He was also aware of a keen intelligence that could be intimidating. Not at all the sort of woman he'd imagined Matthew Armstrong would fall for and stay faithful to for thirty-odd years. More important, she was obviously a good deal older than him, much nearer Brand's own age. She wore her years well, but the bony, liver-spotted hands, the deep lines round the eyes and mouth, the wrinkled neck gave her away.

'What do you think, Mr Brand? The title. *The Sound of Murder*? Very vulgar.'

'We've been through all that, Ella.'

'No, I want to know what Mr Brand thinks.'

Brand scratched his chin. 'Well, it's a bit cheeky, isn't it? Salzburg. *The Sound of Music.*'

'You don't know the film business, old boy,' said Matthew, safe with a subject he understood better than Brand. 'It's a flyer. A full-length movie feature based on *Braddock*. They thought of using that title. But it wouldn't mean anything in the States and that's where the profit is, not in Britain. You can't really blame them for wanting to cash in on a smash hit. Fox are furious, I hear. They made *Music*. But they can't do anything about it.'

'Don't let Matthew fool you, Mr Brand. It's a cheap little cops and robbers movie made by a cheap producer and a novice director. Matthew's worthy of a lot better, a lot better.'

It was a neatly administered hit below the belt. She's had practice, thought Brand. Whether he agreed with her assessment of the film or not, Armstrong rallied to the defence of the three months of his life he was expending on *The Sound of Murder.*

'Ella doesn't rate anything that doesn't measure up to Shakespeare or, at the very least, Tennessee Williams.' Armstrong's laugh had a hollow ring to it.

To defuse the situation, Brand pretended an onlooker's curiosity in a production he already suspected wouldn't light up the heavens—or the box office. 'What's a British police inspector doing in Salzburg? In the film, I mean.'

Retreating into the safety of the character he played, Armstrong expanded on the cleverness of the script and the injection of vitality an American writer had brought to it. 'He—Braddock—has left the force. He's set up as a private eye tracking a mysterious American heiress in Austria.' He had the grace to smile as he said it. 'Put baldly like that I know it sounds pretty silly, but then many film plots do. It's all in the telling. And it widens the horizon, brings in a bankable American name.'

'Judy Clay.' Ella spat out the name as if it had a nasty taste.

'Now, Ella!' There was no mistaking the warning in Armstrong's voice.

But Ella hadn't finished with Judy Clay yet. 'And who gets the star treatment? Who stays in a villa with a swimming pool instead of a second-rate hotel?'

'You know the company aren't picking up the tab, Ella,' he sighed. 'It's her boyfriend's—'

'Lover's—'

'Villa.'

'That slimy old Greek!'

'Well he may be slimy but he's also rich. He's got a villa and she's got him. You can't blame her. I rather like her.'

'You would. You make excuses for everybody. You see, Mr Brand, Matthew won't fight for his rights. He likes to be liked—too much.'

For a moment Brand felt her husband was capable of striking her, but he quickly recovered his easygoing humour, deliberately misinterpreting the comment which was more an accusation than a compliment.

'Well, it's an actor's business to make the public like him.'

She shook her head as at a recalcitrant child. 'You know what I mean,' she said quietly.

'Judy may not be the greatest actress in the world,' he admitted. 'But we've a good back-up cast. Lotte Bruckner. Just a small part, but she'll be magic. Hasn't made a film in years.'

'Now *that's* a star. A light. Like Elisabeth Bergner. Did you ever see her early pictures, Mr Brand? No, I suppose not. She didn't do much outside Europe. Such class! I'm longing to meet her. She's Austrian, you know, like me. Born right here in Salzburg.' It occurred to Brand that these were the first approving words Ella had uttered about anyone or anything connected with the film.

'She starts work tomorrow. There's a lot of local interest,

but she keeps herself very much to herself. Intensely private woman, as they say in the Press, which means she won't go on the Terry Wogan show and won't tell the *Daily Mirror* what she had for breakfast. But then, she doesn't have to. Her reputation precedes her.' Matthew Armstrong was obviously as awestricken at the prospect of working with Lotte Bruckner as his wife was at meeting her.

'I didn't know she was still alive' said Brand. 'I remember seeing her as Anna Karenina, years ago. German or Swedish film. Better than Garbo, I thought. I envy you.'

'I say, Brand. If you're free tomorrow, why don't you come out to the location? We're shooting at a villa near the Bavarian border. You could come out with Ella. Keep her company.'

Even Brand, an outsider, knew such invitations weren't offered lightly. Film units were a clannish lot, not given to welcoming strangers. He wondered whether Armstrong was prompted by more than merely a gesture of friendship. Certainly he brushed aside Brand's suggestion that he might be in the way as of no importance.

'My dear fellow—' an improvement on 'old boy'—'it's hardly a closed set, what with umpteen gawking tourists passing by. I'll clear it with the production office. Ella will be going out about ten. Suit you?'

'Well—if it suits Mrs Armstrong.'

He glanced diffidently at that lady, expecting, even hoping for, an argument. But she smiled at him serenely.

'Ella, please. I'd enjoy your company, Mr Brand.'

Armstrong clapped his hands together. 'Then that's settled. Calls for another drink.'

'Matthew!'

'Well, another time.' Having gained one point, Armstrong conceded this one. 'I think you'll get the flavour of the film. Everyone seems pleased with what we've shot so far. Best of all, the money is pleased.'

'The money?'

'The people who put up the financing. The Television company has the rights and a percentage of the gross, but it's Jake who put the deal together and sold it to the American backers. He thinks they'll be clamouring for a follow-up. Bigger budget. Fingers crossed.'

'And you'll be in it, naturally.'

'Naturally. Jake wants me.'

'But he won't get you—not that easily.' There was no mistaking the determination in Ella's response to her husband's euphoric anticipation of a 'follow-up'. 'This time he got you cheap. Next time he's going to have to pay.'

'Oh come on, Ella, Jake's not so difficult.'

'Jake Schneider is a shit.' Her obscenity silenced the two men. It was uttered quite deliberately for maximum effect, not in the loose-mouthed, meaningless way some film people use foul language. 'Jake Schneider is a shit,' she repeated. 'Just like his father.'

Brand felt deeply uncomfortable. With relief he heard the bartender call his name. 'Inspector Kiesler is waiting in the lobby, sir.'

Never had the cavalry arrived at such an opportune moment, thought Brand.

CHAPTER 3

After the fraught hour Brand had spent in the company of the Armstrongs the evening with his friend Kiesler was doubly pleasurable, a return to a world which wasn't bounded by the current film, the next film and who was getting preferential star treatment.

'Movie people! Crazy people!' Kiesler had been right. Yet, while he found their total self-absorption slightly suffocating, Brand had to admit, for the outsider looking in, they were an intriguing, quixotic group, as unreal as the fantasies they manufactured on the screen. And the threatening undertones he'd sensed in the by-play between Matthew and Ella kept ticking over at the back of Brand's mind, even as he relished the generous hospitality of the Kieslers.

The light, lofty apartment in the suburbs of Salzburg overlooked the river and, after the sudden storm which had thundered round the surrounding hills earlier, the air from their small balcony smelt clean and wholesome.

Maria Kiesler was a plump, fresh-faced woman in her late thirties whose limited English was no impediment to communication. By gesture, deed and the excellence of her cooking—roast veal that melted in the mouth and her own special strudel, '*mit Schlag*,' she'd insisted, ladeling dollops of fluffy cream on the wafer-light pastry—she left Brand in no doubt that he was a welcome guest. She enthused over his gift of Fortnum and Mason's choicest chocolates, even though they were coals to Newcastle in Salzburg where the confectionery was second to none.

Her eyes glowed with a mother's pride as her ten-year-old daughter Leni, allowed up late for a special occasion, bobbed shyly and in painstaking English assured him that she liked school, enjoyed playing the recorder and singing in the choir, but wasn't '*sehr gut*' at arithmetic. With her flaxen hair and happy smile, she was a diminutive replica of her mother: her life predicted in that rosy face. Although, as Brand knew only too well, life had an uneasy habit of confounding its predictions.

He wondered if Ella Armstrong had once been such a child and then wondered why the unbidden thought had occurred to him.

Kiesler's son Kurt watched his sister with the impatient tolerance of an older brother until she was despatched to bed. If Leni seemed part of a fairytale Austria, Kurt was indistinguishable from any other lively adolescent in the Western world who wore jeans and T-shirt as an obligatory uniform, rotated to the rhythm of rock and earnestly lectured

Brand on the evils of modern society—pollution, famine, unemployment, big business and the arms race. Grateful for a willing listener who shared his sentiments if not his youthful passion, he expounded on his favourite subjects between mouthfuls of strudel until his father gently suggested that he might have some unfinished homework.

'The young!' Kiesler smiled as they finished the bottle of good Neuburger. 'Life is so straightforward to the young—method, result and conclusion. All problems can be solved like a mathematical equation. But their instincts are good. It bodes well for the world. Come, Ralph, we can sit on the balcony. It's a mild night and you can smoke that disgusting pipe of yours.' Brand's ever handy pipe and particularly ripe choice of tobacco was a shared joke.

'Frau Kiesler, you'll join us?'

The beaming woman shook her head. 'You go,' she said, shushing them out of the dining-room.

'She'll come later. She thinks we have much to talk about,' Kiesler assured him.

The lights of Salzburg twinkled like stars in the still, night sky as Brand settled his bulky body comfortably in an ample lounger chair.

'I envy you your family, Leo,' he said, acutely conscious that he had none of his own. From this distance his lonely, practical little flat in Sussex seemed even bleaker than it actually was.

Kiesler nodded approvingly. 'They're my sanity. Stop me getting too involved with the job.'

'An occupational hazard.' Brand smiled ruefully.

'*Your* occupational hazard, I think, Ralph. A man shouldn't be alone. You should find some nice, agreeable widow. How about a good Austrian woman? Maria is a great matchmaker.'

Brand chuckled. 'I'm afraid it's too late for all that, Leo. I'd pity any woman who took me on.'

'What's it like being retired?'

'Bags of time on your hands and too little to fill it with. You won't have that trouble when your time comes. You'll have grandchildren. A son with a brilliant career . . .'

'Hold on. It won't be so brilliant if he doesn't attend to his studies more. And little Leni. Who can see into the future? We have problems, even in Salzburg: drugs, dropouts. And the parents are the last to know.'

He seemed surprised at Brand's booming laugh. 'Leo, I can't believe you're serious. Worried about that charming child!'

'You, my friend, are in the throes of love at first sight. I can see the signs.'

'With Leni? Guilty as charged.'

'Not Leni, Ralph. Salzburg! It's the first-time tourists' disease. They see the city of light and roses and Mozart, with its well-preserved buildings, friendly people and good food. And they think: That's all there is. They can't believe that the life, the anxieties, the animosities they've left behind exist here too. We weren't always such a happy city. Remember we're only a few miles from Berchtesgaden and many Austrians welcomed Hitler as a hero.'

'But that's history, Leo.'

'Not so historical. There are still some who have cause to remember—for one reason or another.'

'That's true of everywhere in Europe. England, America, too. But forty, fifty years is a long time.'

With a visible effort, Kiesler shrugged off his moody introspection. He was a courteous host and whatever had sparked it off he mustn't allow it to cloud Brand's visit.

'You're right, Ralph. It's a long time ago. I can't think what made me bring it up. You're on holiday and you must enjoy all this.' He waved at the scene below him. 'I shall take some time off. I'm due a few days. But meanwhile, what are your plans?'

He was the old Kiesler again.

'You'll hardly believe it, but I'm going out to the film location tomorrow.'

'For fun?' Kiesler was duly amazed. The film unit had been nothing but trouble for him, but then trouble was his job.

'I've been invited.'

Brand related the events that had led up to Armstrong's suggestion that he watch the film in production, embellishing it with humour here and there, the better to relish Kiesler's hearty laughter.

'What did I tell you? They're mad. What a welcome to receive on your arrival in our city. To be ticked off for being late as a stray actor. Still, it's good to have run into a friend. This man—Matthew Armstrong. Of course, we know him. We've seen the Television series, dubbed into German. But I can't say I recognized my old colleague Ralph Brand in the character.'

'Neither could I. But Armstrong was very insistent.'

'He sounds a very insistent man.'

Brand frowned. 'Oddly enough, he isn't. Except—he did seem to want me to go out to the set. I wonder . . .'

'Now you're sounding like a detective. He probably just likes you. If that were a crime, Maria and I would stand indicted.'

But as Kiesler drove him back to the hotel after he'd thanked Maria profusely for her fine meal, Brand couldn't rid himself of the feeling that the actor's motive was somewhat stronger than the mere fact that he'd liked the cut of his jib.

Behind the reception desk Fritz Sommer was still on duty. Exchanging his brass-buttoned hunting green jacket for black linen was his only concession to the lateness of the hour.

'Don't you ever sleep, Fritz?'

'In the tourist season, Herr Brand, we never sleep. It's a luxury reserved for the winter.' He handed Brand his key with the trace of a comradely smile.

Several hours later, after picking at half a croissant and draining a pot of black coffee (the Neuburger had had more of a kick than it seemed on first tasting), Brand was idling his time in the lobby waiting for Ella Armstrong when Debbie Price raced down the stairs, preceded by a large, loose-limbed man with a peevish look and a bulging brief-case.

He was muttering angrily something about cooperation —or, more likely, the lack of it. 'Never worked on such a disorganized movie,' he flung over his shoulder at the breathless production coordinator. 'All these locations were sorted out and properly authorized weeks ago. Then Barry sees somewhere pretty and wants to shoot it. That's what comes of having a whizzkid whose only experience of direct-ing a film is TV commercials.'

Debbie Price's attempt at placating noises petered out in a familiar grumble: 'Well, don't take it out on me. I just work here.' She caught sight of Brand, registering some faint recognition.

'Are you Matthew's friend? You're going out on the location with Ella, he said. Where is that—' she looked around the lobby and ended feelingly—'woman?'

Brand acknowledged her recognition, he hoped win-ningly. 'You've found the contact lens, then.'

She peered at him more closely. 'They called in a plumber. I didn't get your name?'

'Well, it isn't Jeremy Fox,' Brand teased her.

She screwed up her nose, apparently puzzled. Jeremy Fox was yesterday's problem already superseded by today's.

'Ralph Brand,' he relented.

'That's right. I remember now.' He doubted whether she had.

'Well, come on. I haven't got all day. Where is she?' The man with the peevish look humped his briefcase from one hand to the other.

'Keep your hair on. I'll find her.' Remembering her manners, Debbie Price effected a cursory introduction. 'This is Murray Pick, our location manager. He'll be sharing your car.'

The man grunted a greeting, not unfriendly but hardly reassuring. Actors' entourages weren't his business. They were just added nuisance value.

'Have I kept you waiting?'

They all turned round at the sound of Ella Armstrong's trilling voice. She stepped out of the lift. Her immaculate appearance in sleek-fitting slacks and Jaeger sweater contrasted noticeably with the ruffled inelegance of the workers. There was no hint of apology or urgency in her tone. She might have been keeping a late appointment with her hairdresser or dressmaker.

Brand smiled. Debbie Price sighed. But Murray Pick eyed her coldly and deliberately turned his back.

'My dear Debbie, was it *absolutely* necessary to call my husband for seven this morning, when he isn't in the first shot?' Ella smiled sweetly and lethally at the girl.

'I just type the call sheets, I don't make them up.'

Brand felt he could have cut the antagonism in the lobby with a knife. Interesting! He could understand Debbie Price's exasperation with the demanding Ella, but what had Murray Pick against her?

'I'll sit in front,' said the location manager as he took his seat beside the driver in the car. He nodded politely at Brand and pointedly ignored Ella.

As they left behind the already bustling streets of Salzburg and drove into the countryside, Brand noticed discreet roadside signs with an arrow and the title *The Sound of Murder*.

'They certainly advertise the film, don't they?' he said, realizing it was probably an inane remark. But it broke the heavy silence.

'This is nothing,' said Pick. 'I was working in the hills

above Almería once when they were shooting three Westerns at the same time. It was like Piccadilly Circus.'

'What happened?'

'The Indians from one Western got mixed up with the cowboys from another and the star on the third movie had it off with an extra in his caravan while they sorted out the mess.'

'And did they sort out the mess?'

'Depends what you mean by mess. The extra got pregnant and slapped a paternity suit on the star. One director had a nervous breakdown, another won an Oscar and the third went into Television. I believe *he's* having a nervous breakdown now.'

'But the films got made.'

'Oh, they always do. In the end. Can't think how, sometimes. It's usually a photo-finish.'

Brand chuckled. 'That's really funny. Movies! Photo-finish.'

The location manager didn't see the joke. Explaining the apparent chaos of movie-making to an outsider was like trying to teach a three-year-old the theory of relativity.

Ella seemed unconcerned that she wasn't included in this exchange. She moved closer to Brand in the back seat. He was aware of those clever eyes appraising him.

'You know, Mr Brand, Ralph—I may call you Ralph?— you have an actor's profile, clean and positive. I'm not surprised they mistook you for one.'

Brand felt foolish and flattered at the same time. 'Only because of an errant contact lens.'

'Have you ever been on the stage? An amateur perhaps?'

'Very amateur. I played Puck once in school. Tripped over my loincloth on my first entrance.'

Her trilling laugh caused a shudder in the broad back in front of him. 'How can you trip over a loincloth?'

'The teacher forgot to tuck in the ends when she shoved

me on stage, quaking with fright. I knew then I wasn't
destined for the theatre.'

'Did you know Matthew very well? That time in Worthing?' she asked suddenly.

Brand thought back. He could only be honest. 'I didn't
think so at the time.'

'He does. It's surprising. Matthew is quite gregarious,
but deep down he doesn't take easily to people. I don't know
what impression you took away from our meeting last night.'

Brand decided against honesty this time. 'I—I didn't
take any particular impression away.'

'Come now, you must have thought I was a little—how
can I put it?—over-protective.' Graciously put, but not
quite accurate, thought Brand.

'You know, Matthew is a simple man, Ralph. He was a
simple boy, a simple young man and now a simple middle-
aged man. He sees and feels only what he wants to see and
feel. And he's easily persuadable. I have to counter that—
for his sake.'

Again, that laugh, like the chirruping of an insistent bird
at dawn, echoed round the car.

'I remember when I first met him. . .'

The location manager turned round abruptly. 'Do you
mind if I open the window.' It was a statement not a
question. 'It's stuffy in here.'

Brand, surprised and none too warm, reluctantly indicated he had no objection. After all, he was a guest. Ella
wasn't asked for an opinion.

As an unseasonably chill wind from the mountains
whistled through the open window Brand noticed that
Murray Pick was shivering, but not, he sensed, from the
cold.

CHAPTER 4

The villa where *The Sound of Murder* was shooting was a graceful, cream-stuccoed, late Hapsburg building set squarely in a small park. Normally, it was a haven of peace tucked away in the hills above Salzburg. But not today. The owners, having exacted generous compensation from the film company for the use of it, had wisely decided to take an extended vacation. When they returned they would find it in the same immaculate order in which they had left it. Production companies scrupulously honour the terms of the contract whereby they're required to leave the property in the condition they found it.

Meanwhile it looked as if a demolition gang had hit it. Arc lights, cranes and cameras cluttered the drive to the house. In the clearing by what might once have been stables, caravans, trucks and catering vans were parked. Battalions of technicians, carpenters, prop men, hairdressers, wardrobe assistants, a British and an Austrian crew dovetailing duties not always amicably, produced a cacophony of noise, punctuated by barked orders and the occasional expletive in two languages.

The Austrians all seemed to be named 'Ernst' or 'Karl' and the British 'Mike', 'Dave' and 'Fred'. Particularly Fred. Even the pretty girl Brand had noticed the previous evening, now steering one visiting journalist out of camera range and around the cables that littered the gravel path, was named Fred. The other journalist was huddled with whom Brand took to be the whizzkid director, who was earnestly explaining that he was creating a '*film noir*' in colour, an impressionist *Double Indemnity*, a Renoir-esque *Big Sleep*.' The journalist nodded sagely and scribbled down the quote for his piece in *Sight and Sound*.

In a canvas chair with his name stamped on the back, Matthew Armstrong was having a small wound on his forehead blooded up by a serious young woman with a make-up box. The director paused in the middle of describing just how he proposed to make a black and white film in colour to yell, 'Don't mask the eyes.'

Armstrong spotted Brand, waved and beckoned, causing a splodge of 'blood' to trickle down his cheek. The make-up girl patiently mopped it up. 'Head up, Matt.'

Brand threaded his way through the crowds and hardware to cries of 'Watch it, mate' as one of the Freds narrowly missed clouting him with a plank of wood.

'Not what you expected, old boy?' said Armstrong, his head clamped in position as his wound grew rosier under the make-up girl's deft fingers. 'Glamorous life, we lead. Up at six, daubed up like a clown and spend most of the day doing the crossword for thirty seconds on the screen.' He didn't make it sound like a hard life.

'You know you love it,' said the girl. She stood back and surveyed her handiwork. 'That should meet with his majesty's approval.'

'How's it going, Matt?'

The corpulent man with the bald head and the cast in one eye, who had been subjected to Ella's tirade about accommodation in the hotel lobby the day before, loomed up behind the actor's chair and gripped his shoulders with surprisingly thin, impeccably manicured fingers.

'Just great, Jake. You haven't met my old friend, Ralph Brand, have you?' In twenty-four hours Brand seemed to have been elevated from a casual acquaintance to a buddy of long standing in Armstrong's estimation.

'My pleasure, Mr Brand.' Schneider's handshake was as sincere as his hearty Californian greeting. The altercation with Armstrong's wife appeared to have been forgotten just as Debbie Price had forgotten she'd mistaken Brand for Jeremy Fox. He supposed film units had short memories.

Either that or they stored them up for future reference.

'It's kind of you to let me . . .'

'Nonsense. Any friend of Matt's is welcome. Which is more than I can say for some visitors.' Brand followed his eyes, which were focused on Ella who was deep in conversation with the girl named Fred.

'A word, Matt. I'd like you to do a run-through with Lotte. She's a bit iffy—' the director rotated his right hand palm down—'know what I mean? First film in years.' Having wrenched himself away from his vision of what the movie might be, he was now busying himself with actually getting it made.

'Sure thing, Barry. This is Ralph Brand, old friend. Barry Butler, our young genius director.' The director winced, nodded briefly at Brand and paid him no attention.

Jake Schneider put his arm round Brand's shoulders, which didn't seem called for. Schneider, Brand judged, was a toucher who never really felt he was communicating with anyone unless flesh met flesh.

'They're setting up a shot between Matt and Lotte Bruckner. Great *coup* for us, getting her. She's turned down dozens of scripts. But I managed to persuade her to do this one. It's a beautiful little role. She'll be perfect. This old, strange countess from the past who's been sheltering the heiress. I suppose Matt's told you a bit about the plot? But she's nervous. Understandably. Born in Salzburg, feels the old pull. But not too happy working on home ground.'

Brand felt some response was required.

'She's a fine actress. I'll enjoy seeing her acting again.' But he needn't have bothered himself. Schneider's conversations were invariably one-sided, unless he was confronted by an Ella.

'We've high hopes for this one.' Lotte Bruckner and her nerves were already forgotten. 'They say I'm crazy on the coast.'

'Coast?'

Schneider looked surprised, as if unable to credit that anyone couldn't know what coast he was talking about. 'Hollywood. L.A. "Who wants to see a movie about a British shamus in Austria," they said. But when I saw Matt's TV series I knew better. I've got a nose. The fans are ready for a return to a good, old-fashioned movie. Spielberg's had his day. Kids' stuff,' he went on, dismissing the most successful film-maker in the world with a wave of his hand. 'Chemistry, that's what they want. Star chemistry. I knew Matt had it. But I couldn't see how I could make him acceptable to the Middle West. Then I thought of Judy Clay. Young, blonde, sassy, very American. Complete opposites. That's chemistry.'

Brand extricated himself politely from the producer's grip. 'I see what you mean,' he said, though he doubted whether he did. He conceded he was no expert, but Armstrong had seemed to him just another workmanlike actor who'd had a lucky break, while Judy Clay had featured more often in the gossip columns than in any particularly memorable movies. Still, who was he to dampen the producer's enthusiasm?

He was about to make some further innocuous remark when he realized that Schneider had already deserted him and was engaged in some technical discussion with the location manager who was looking increasingly disgruntled. Brand looked around for a friendly, or at least recognizable face, found none and perched on the low granite wall that skirted the drive to the villa. He had just decided that film-making was ninety per cent boredom and ten per cent frenzy when he was brusquely commanded to find another home. 'Get him out of there, Mike,' said a loud voice from behind the camera.

A slim young man in a puffer jacket, presumably Mike, hurried over to Brand. 'Sorry, chum, you'll have to move. You'll be in shot.'

'I thought it seemed too peaceful here.' Brand removed

himself and wondered how he could decently return to the relative sanity of Salzburg, if, indeed, there were any transport to take him. He doubted that he'd be missed.

'You're safer behind the camera.' He felt himself being propelled back into the mêlée on the drive towards a couple of upturned boxes. 'Might as well take the weight off our feet. They'll be ages yet.'

Brand turned to thank his rescuer and found himself face to face with his look-alike Jeremy Fox, who was daubed with dirt and heavily scarred. The make-up department had obviously been busy that morning.

'You look in a bad way,' chuckled Brand.

'Fatal. I'm the murderer. They're topping me off today.'

'So you'll be going back to London?'

'Heavens, no. I've got my scenes to do tomorrow and the next day.'

'But you'll be dead.'

The actor gave him a quizzical look. 'Don't know much about film-making, do you? They don't shoot in sequence. I've still got to do poor old Arthur's scenes they had to scrap when he had the heart attack. Not much, just a bit of menace. Glad when it's all over, though. Give me a nice spot on telly any day. Close to home, sleep in your own bed at night. Still, it's a good little earner. Live on expenses and bank the salary and they upped the ante because they needed someone quickly.'

The make-up girl came fussing over. 'Barry doesn't like that chest wound.'

'Neither do I,' said the actor feelingly.

'I've got to mess it up a bit. You'd better come over to the light where I can do a proper job on it.'

'Duty calls.' Jeremy Fox sighed and followed the girl at a quick trot. Brand watched his companion leave with a sinking feeling. Alone again. Ella and Armstrong were nowhere in sight. Schneider had forgotten him and the location manager didn't want to know. Feeling decidedly spare, he sauntered around to the rear of the villa past the parked vans, trucks and cars, fairly sure that he was no longer 'in shot'.

After the chaos in the drive at the front it seemed unnaturally quiet, the house providing a barrier against the noise. Brand looked around him appreciatively. He felt as if he'd wandered into another, graceful world. The sweeping lawns hedged with floribundas sloped down to a lily-pond and a summerhouse—not a frivolous folly but a good, substantial structure—nestled underneath the trees.

If he closed his eyes he could imagine it as it might have been on a lazy summer evening in the twilight of the Hapsburg empire with ladies in long lace dresses and upright men in uniforms flirting and sipping champagne to the strains of Strauss filtering through the open French windows. 'Sentimental old fool,' he chided himself. He remembered Kiesler's warning. It was easy to fall prey to the tourists' disease here. Easy to surrender to the charm of the place, to bask in the rosy glow of a past which probably hadn't been anything like his imagining.

He walked towards the summerhouse, at first furtively, then with more confidence when no angry minion ordered him back whence he came. As he approached it he thought it was empty. But then he heard voices. Through the window he saw it had been fitted out as a kind of dressing-room. A woman with her back to him was gazing into a mirror as a hairdresser nervously teased her hair into an elegant chignon. She was dressed in a flowing tea-gown high at the neck. The face in the mirror was unmistakably that of Lotte Bruckner, much aged since he'd last seen her on the screen but still commanding, the skin stretched tautly over the marvellous cheekbones. But the face wore a curious expression, part disbelief, part anger. It wasn't directed at the hairdresser, but at a woman in the corner who was prattling on apparently unaware of the reaction she was provoking.

Conscious that he was eavesdropping, Brand was about

to beat a silent retreat when he identified the voice of the prattling woman. It was Ella Armstrong. The snatches of her conversation that Brand caught seemed innocuous enough, hardly warranting the by now venomous response she was getting from Lotte Bruckner. 'Had to meet you— so admired . . . both from Salzburg . . . little village near here . . . Grinzing . . .' Brand had obviously come in on the tail-end of the conversation.

The hairdresser, catching the look reflected in the mirror, was making frantic signs to Ella to leave, but she continued unconcerned until Lotte Bruckner turned, her eyes blazing.

'Get that woman out of here,' she said. She spoke quietly, but the effect couldn't have been more electrifying if she'd roared out loud. Out of the corner of his eye, Brand saw Jake Schneider, with the assistant director Mike in tow, pacing towards the summerhouse. If he noticed Brand, he didn't comment.

'My darling Lotte. Ready when you are,' he said effusively. Then he stopped when he saw Ella. 'Now, Ella . . .' he started to say with a touch of exasperation.

'Get that woman out of here,' Lotte Bruckner repeated implacably.

Ella backed away, a baffled expression on her face. 'I was only being . . . as we're both from this region . . . I thought . . .' Her excuses petered out.

'For God's sake, Ella, what have you been saying to her?' Schneider muttered.

As she left the summerhouse, Brand almost felt sorry for her. There were tears in her eyes, less of sorrow than of bemusement, as if she genuinely hadn't understood why or how she'd offended the actress. Not wanting to add to her humiliation by letting her feel she'd been observed, Brand move noiselessly out of sight to the back of the wooden structure.

When he heard the door shut firmly, he came out of his hiding place and watched the regal procession cross the lawn towards the French windows: Lotte Bruckner, flanked by Schneider, a supporting hand on her elbow, the assistant director, with the hairdresser bringing up the rear. In the distance he could see Barry Butler and Matthew Armstrong anxiously waiting.

If he'd had any doubts before who 'that damned woman' was Brand had none now. Ella Armstrong had an uncommon knack of rubbing everyone up the wrong way. But whatever it was between her and Lotte Bruckner was more deep-seated than mere irritation and he'd have sworn that Ella hadn't the slightest idea what had caused it.

He made his way back to the front of the villa where Barry Butler was in earnest consultation with Lotte and Matthew, placing them on their marks by the open front door.

'We'll just have a run through. Let's have quiet, everybody.'

The set fell instantly silent, all eyes on Lotte. Everyone knew they were in the presence of a cinema legend and a legend demanded respect.

Haltingly the actress mouthed her lines as the camera dollied in on her. 'Herr Braddock, you're trespassing.' She stopped suddenly.

'You've no right to invade my privacy,' prompted the continuity girl, squatting beside Barry Butler.

'You've no right . . .' The actress stopped again and turned to Barry. 'I can't,' she said in her normal voice. 'I must speak with you and Schneider.'

Barry Butler threw up his arms. 'All right, everybody. We'll take a lunch-break.'

He bounded towards Lotte but Schneider was there first. Matthew Armstrong looked puzzled, excluded from the conference.

The crew were making their way to the catering vans and the trestle tables laid out beside them. No one was claiming any responsibility for Brand, until the location manager

Murray Pick came up behind him. 'Hungry? You'd better come with me.'

As they queued in line, Brand noticed that the Austrians chose smoked pork and sauerkraut while the British to a man opted for lamb chops and two veg.

'Don't they prefer to sample the local food?' he asked Murray Pick.

'Good Lord, no. A British crew expect to eat what they know on location. And if you'd suffered Delhi belly in India or dysentery up the Amazon on a film, I can tell you *you'd* be grateful for chips with everything.'

Brand was about to help himself to the smoked pork when he felt a tug at his arm.

'Thought I'd lost you, old boy. We're eating up at the house with the grown-ups.' It was Matthew Armstrong. But he obviously didn't have food on his mind.

'Look, it's a bit embarrassing, but would you mind taking Ella back to the hotel after lunch? No, she doesn't want any. She's waiting in the car. Seems—difficult to say really. Can't understand it. I know she can be pushy. All the same.'

'All the same, what?'

'Well, it seems Lotte won't work with Ella around. Bit ga-ga, I think. Probably nothing. But—well, would you mind, awfully?'

'Of course not, I'd be delighted. Feel a bit of an outsider anyway.' Brand smiled reassuringly. The man's embarrassment was painful to witness. 'I'll go now if you like. Not all that hungry. Maybe we could have a bite back at the hotel.'

Armstrong heaved a sigh of relief. 'That's a weight off my mind. Ella likes you. I'm sure it's all a storm in a teacup, blow over in no time.' He paused as if not quite sure whether he should push his luck.

'There is one other little favour,' he said finally. 'You don't suppose you could sort of look after Ella tomorrow? Keep her off the location.'

'Lotte Bruckner?' It seemed logical.

'Not exactly, old boy. Just, you'd be doing me a favour. I won't forget it. Maybe you could take in a little excursion. Ella'd like to show you some of the sights and I never get the time.'

Brand nodded. After all, he'd nothing to lose and his curiosity had been whetted. He was beginning to understand why Armstrong was so chummy. For some reason he wanted his wife out of the way tomorrow and it wasn't only because of her clash with Lotte Bruckner.

CHAPTER 5

Ella didn't look up when he got into the car beside her. She sat huddled in the corner, nursing her grievance. She seemed suddenly smaller, older, far less assured.

As he shut the door, her husband made a helpless gesture for Brand's benefit. 'See you later, my dear. Envy you— lovely day like this! Who wants to be cooped up on a film set?' His attempt at jocularity fell dismally flat. He sounded like any middle-class, middle-aged husband not quite sure how to placate a wife who complained he spent all his Sundays attending to business. Not for the first time, Brand was amazed that this rather ordinary, ineffectual man could be transformed by the camera into a charismatic hero. He wondered whether Paul Newman or Robert Redford or Roger Moore were as personally unexceptional in the privacy of the home. He somehow doubted it.

Yet maybe he was just being taken in by another acting performance. It was clear that Matthew Armstrong had his secrets, perhaps even a secret life.

They drove for several miles in silence, for which Brand was grateful. It had been an instructive morning and the detective in him relished the time in which to organize his thoughts.

As they approached the outskirts of the city, Ella's mood visibly lightened as if she'd decided to shrug off as too trivial to be dwelt upon the ugly incident that had caused her explusion from the set.

'It's so good of you to accompany me, Ralph. I hate being driven alone. Such a bore on the location, didn't you think? I couldn't bear to stay a moment longer.'

She affected the manner of some silly, empty-headed woman with a butterfly mind, which Brand knew she wasn't.

But then he realized the façade was deliberate, her way of soothing the hurt Lotte Bruckner had inexplicably inflicted.

She'd assumed that Matthew hadn't told Brand the reason for her abrupt departure and he didn't disillusion her.

She chattered amiably, pointing out places of interest, reminiscing about the changes that had taken place since she was a girl. It seemed as good a moment as any to broach the subject of that little excursion Matthew had proposed for the next day. While feeling himself being used for purposes he couldn't yet fathom, Brand was aware that he didn't really mind. For all her irritating ways, her quicksilver changes of mood, Ella was an intriguing 'case' and Brand never could resist a good case. His old colleague, Sergeant now Inspector John Waller, would have recognized the signs and cautioned him. 'Don't get involved, keep your distance, first rule of police training.' But Waller wasn't there. He was plodding away, keeping law and order in Sussex.

'That's the trouble with being a tourist. You need a native to show you around,' he said tentatively.

'Well, I'm hardly a native any more. I haven't been back since I left before the war as a girl. But, of course, if you'd like . . .'

'I would. My friend on the force here has his job. I can hardly impose too much on his time. I'm free tomorrow. If you are.'

She was studying him carefully with those damnably

acute eyes, weighing his words, assessing his reasons. He felt that his mind was being stripped naked. Subterfuges didn't wash with Ella.

'Matthew put you up to this, didn't he? Don't answer. I know he did. Well, what does it matter?! It hasn't mattered for a long time.' She was silent again for a few moments. If she refused, he'd done his best and Matthew Armstrong could lump it. It was his problem, whatever it was, not Brand's.

He looked out of the window at the passing parade of tourists. Then surprisingly he heard a throaty chuckle from the small figure beside him.

'I think it would be amusing' she said. 'We could have breakfast and make plans.' The chuckle subsided. 'We outsiders have to stick together, don't we.' The strange remark didn't call for an answer even if Brand could have thought of one, and it didn't sound all that amusing.

She refused his offer of lunch, pleading a headache, and Brand was left to his own devices for the rest of the day. He decided to stay clear of the hotel until much later. He'd had enough of film units for twenty-four hours. He booked a seat for the Marionette Theatre in the evening and watched the puppets miming *The Marriage of Figaro* from a hard seat which gave him limited vision of the stage. The famous puppets, he decided, were overrated. He closed his eyes and hoped the recorded music of Mozart's most ebullient opera would lift his spirits. But his mind kept returning to Ella's odd comment: 'we outsiders have to stick together.' It wasn't so unsettling, the sort of thing people say in passing. But Ella had meant it and he wondered why.

The next morning she was as brisk and chipper as she'd appeared on their first meeting, in charge of the situation.

'So, where first?'

'I've an admission,' said Brand. 'You probably won't like it, too touristy.'

'But that's what we are—tourists!'

'I've always wanted to do an excursion to *The Sound of Music* locations.'

'You *are* mad.' But she didn't seem too put out. 'We'll hire a car, every driver in Salzburg knows where to go. Leopoldskron, Mondsee . . .'

'Would you mind very much if we actually took one of the excursions on a coach with a guide?'

'With all those dreadful American matrons, oohing and aahing and singing "Edelweiss"?'

'Well—' he borrowed her own phrase—'it might be amusing.'

'You *are* a character, Ralph Brand. Matthew said you were, and for once he was right.'

But she allowed herself to be persuaded. The ever-present Fritz on the desk was his usual helpful self. Of course he could book places on the tour. They left every two hours.

As he busied himself on the telephone Ella hummed the theme song softly. 'This will take me back. The route goes near my village, Grinzing. Can you imagine I was born a peasant, a little Austrian peasant?' Yes, thought Brand, I can imagine that. It explained a lot about Ella.

'I've no family, of course. They're long dead. I can't tell you how glad I was to leave that place and even more glad to lose my name. My surname. Knödel. Do you know what *knödel* means in English? Dumpling! Ella Dumpling!' He realized as she laughed, remembering, that she must have been an enchanting girl.

'The tickets are booked, Herr Brand. You pick up the coach at the Mirabellplatz.'

The head porter looked from Brand to Ella, an interested expression on his normally deadpan face. Perhaps he suspects a liaison, thought Brand. Well, hardly, with a coachload of Ella's 'dreadful' American matrons looking on.

Once on the coach, Brand couldn't think why he'd wanted to make the trip in the first place. Second childhood, he supposed. The company was even more intimidating for a

mere male than Ella had warned him it might be. By chance
they'd joined the ladies' floral society from Sacramento
whose members, Canon Sureshots at the ready, were determined to get maximum value from every moment of their
whistle-stop package tour of Europe.

He was one of only two men on the coach: the other, a
disgruntled American husband who obviously wished he
were somewhere else, buried himself in a lurid paperback
and refused to surface for the entire trip. Conscious of thirty
pairs of curious eyes following him up the aisle of the coach,
Brand sank into a back seat beside Ella, fumbled for his
pipe and was about to pack it with tobacco when a shrill,
friendly voice in front pointed out: '*Rauchen Verboten!*
Naughty!' Feeling like a schoolboy who'd misbehaved at his
mother's tea-party, he shrank further into his seat.

Cupping her mouth with her hand Ella mimicked the
reprimand precisely under her breath: '*Rauchen Verboten!*
Naughty! I told you so.' But she seemed to be enjoying
herself hugely, chatting with the ladies, adding her own
comments to those of the chummy guide and joining in *The
Sound of Music* choruses that were played incessantly on tape
during the trip. Everyone, it seemed, knew the words.

Dragging a reluctant Brand by the hand, she was first off
the coach when they alighted at Leopoldskron castle—
which had masqueraded as the Trapp family home in the
film—for a photo stop. She leaned on the railing admiring
its glittering, baroque reflection in the lake that fronted the
building. Sounding like dozens of snapping fingers, the
cameras clicked around her.

'Blanche,' trilled the lady who had ticked Brand off for
brandishing his pipe, 'have you ever seen anything more
darling?'

Blanche being otherwise engaged with a shutter that
didn't work, she turned to Ella. 'Isn't it just darling?'

'Yes, it's darling,' Ella repeated. Her eyes misted over.
'Max Reinhardt lived there,' she said softly.

Blanche's friend puckered her lips, certain that she should know the name but not sure that she did. 'Reinhardt. I seem to recall . . .'

'He was the master. A great theatrical impresario. He staged the most lavish productions of Mozart at the Salzburg Festivals. He wasn't so well known in America. Although he did make a film there, *A Midsummer Night's Dream.*'

The puzzled face cleared. 'Of *course*. I saw it on Television not long ago. Mickey Rooney, James Cagney.'

'That's the one. But it was here that he was revered. A long time ago. Then he had to leave. Like they all did.'

'All?' said Brand, moved by the obviously deep emotion she was experiencing.

'The artists. The Jews. From 1933. Already in Berlin and later in Vienna they were calling him "the Jew Goldman". That was his real name. I worked for him, you know.' She shrugged and smiled. 'Oh, just a tiny cog in a giant wheel. I was an apprentice seamstress on one of his last productions here. I was just fourteen. That's one thing the nuns taught me, how to sew neatly. So long, so long ago.'

She looked up at Brand, but her eyes didn't see him. They were focused on some distant memory of the past when she couldn't have imagined what life had in store for her. He felt suddenly strongly protective as if she were in fact that fourteen-year-old girl from the country wide-eyed with wonder at her first glimpse of the sophisticated world of Reinhardt and those others who had to leave.

They were interrupted by the guide clapping hands, anxious to keep to his schedule. 'Ready, ladies! We're leaving for Mondsee where we'll take a lunch-break.' He spoke English with an acquired American accent in quick bursts, like a sprinter eager to breast the tape before his breath ran out.

It was a good ten minutes before he'd rounded up his flock and herded them back on to the coach, admonishing a blushing Blanche for keeping the others waiting. 'There's always one,' he murmured to Brand, man to man.

Ella barely spoke on the drive to Mondsee. It was a reflective silence, not bitter but oddly uncomfortable for her, Brand sensed. He listened idly to the guide's rapid spurts of information over the loudspeaker. 'In the church at Mondsee, Maria married von Trapp . . . you'll remember the scene, with Julie Andrews and Christopher Plummer . . .' Thirty heads bobbed in unison. The actors had already robbed the real-life family who had fled from the Nazis of their identity.

'Matthew was a splendid von Trapp once,' Ella said suddenly. 'Oh, years ago. It was a summer season in one of those dreadful resorts in the north, Bridlington or Blackpool. He hadn't the voice, alas, but great authority. I coached him. Terrible production, though. Such a waste!' Unable to think of a suitable comment Brand kept quiet and admired the scenery.

The rolling meadows, lakes and wooded slopes of the mountains, with doll's house chalets nestling in sudden clearings, sped by more or less unnoticed and the sound of music echoed round the coach from thirty variously tuneful or tuneless voices.

At the village of Mondsee the members of the floral society traipsed round the courtyard of the church with their cameras vowing that they 'couldn't eat a bite'. Ella found an unassuming little café off the main street with an inviting vacant table under an awning over the pavement. 'I don't know if you've had enough of the sound of music, but *I* have —besides I'm ravenous.' Brand agreed with alacrity. 'You can go off a movie.' He was already regretting that he hadn't accepted Ella's suggestion that they hire a car.

As she studied the menu, Brand studied her. It was a different Ella sitting opposite him across the checked tablecloth. Mellow, compassionate, but troubled. He'd seen her tough and abrasive with Jake Schneider; a fussy mother hen to her husband; destroyed, for whatever reason, by Lotte Bruckner. Yet she always seemed to bounce back with a new persona to surprise him. He marvelled at the many facets of this extraordinary woman who wore her years so lightly, as if they were a statistic of no consequence. He supposed it had something to do with the diversity of her life. Most of the women he'd known had been earthbound, living their lives in a well tilled furrow. Using the same analogy, Ella Armstrong was a bird, free soaring, resilient to the buffetting of nature.

Having ordered a frugal meal for a ravenous appetite, she commented on his speculative inspection of her. 'So, what's the verdict?' He lowered his eyes, embarrassed at being caught out.

'You think I'm an odd one, don't you, Brand? I have trouble with Ralph. Brand suits you better. Well?'

'Yes, but I wouldn't say odd, exactly. Interesting, perhaps.'

'I'm glad you're interested, because I want your opinion about something.' Her nervous fingers crushed a pretzel, then she scattered the morsels on the pavement and watched a bird peck at them warily.

'About what? My opinion?'

'What kind of a detective were you, are you? Facts or instinct?'

To anyone but Brand it would have seemed a curious question, but he knew very well what she meant. 'Facts *and* instinct.' He thought back to his years on the force. 'Mostly instinct,' he admitted wryly. 'It used to get me into a lot of trouble sometimes with my superiors.'

She smiled. 'That's what I imagined. So you'll understand what I'm going to say. I have—how can I put it?—a strange feeling I'm being watched. No, watched isn't even the right word. It's as if someone, don't ask me who, is weighing me up, observing me—a bit like you've been observing me— waiting for me to do or say something so that they can be certain, but I've no idea of what. Does that make any kind of sense?'

Even Brand, who had spent his working life evaluating the hidden fears and guilts of human beings, couldn't grasp what she was trying to say.

She caught his puzzled look and anticipated his first logical response. 'Oh, I don't mean the usual nosiness of a film unit. I know how they tend to regard me, a busybody where Matthew's concerned, a nuisance. I'm used to that. It doesn't bother me, never has. It's something else, something I can't explain even to myself—so how can I explain it to you? It's as if . . . No, really, it's too absurd. I don't know why I brought it up.'

'But whatever it is, whoever it is, worries you.'

'More than worries me, Brand.' She looked at him steadily and he saw in her eyes something he'd hoped he'd never see again after he'd retired from the police. Ella Armstrong was frightened. Underneath all those faces she put on for public view, she was deeply scared. The more so because it was a fear of the unknown, the inexplicable.

'You don't think it's absurd?'

He shook his head. 'I think it's very real because you're too practical a woman to invent phantoms.'

'Then at least you don't think I'm going mad.' It was a poor joke and she couldn't sustain her attempt at a dismissive laugh. 'Come on, let's enjoy our lunch.'

CHAPTER 6

In the event neither of them was capable of enjoying lunch. Ella was preoccupied, Brand disturbed on her account. As they picked over the food that deserved more justice than they could do to it, he abandoned any attempt to jolly her out of her suspicions. Instead he urged her to talk about herself. Although not in so many words, she'd pleaded for help and the only way he could begin to help was to know her better, to try to discover where that nameless phantom might be lurking. And he couldn't ignore the coincidence that her sudden fear should be provoked on this return to her roots in the Salzburger Land—any more, perhaps, than she could.

'Strange, coming back,' she mused. 'You know, it's almost fifty years. It's so different. Yet, why should I feel it's still the same?'

'I don't suppose Salzburg has changed that much since you were a girl. Just superficially. Haven't you ever wanted to return before?'

'No, never,' she said firmly. 'I didn't want to come back this time. It was just the film—and Matthew.'

He watched her peel and dissect a pear neatly, no mess, no sticky fingers: the simple operation planned and precise, much, he imagined, as she'd organized her life.

'Did you hate it here, so much?' he prompted.

She considered the question for a moment. 'Hate's a hard word,' she said finally. 'No, I didn't hate it. I felt stifled. I didn't belong. Even as a girl I knew there was a great, wide world outside waiting for me. I just had to find a way of reaching it.'

'And what about your family, your parents? Did they understand?'

She shoved the plate with the remains of the peeled pear away from her impatiently. 'How could they? Grinzing, my village, was their home, their cocoon. They'd lived there all their lives, as *their* parents and grandparents had lived there. They couldn't conceive why anyone should want to escape.

'My father was the village carpenter, my mother kept chickens, grew vegetables, baked pies and raised children. He was dour, she was bovine,' she went on bitterly. 'There was precious little of that famous Austrian *Gemütlichkeit* in our home. No poetry, no music, no fun. I doubt whether my parents said one unnecessary word to each other all their lives. If they were fond of each other or us they never showed it. At least, that's how it seemed to me then. I wonder. Children can be so cruel, so blinkered.'

Maybe for the first time she seemed to be examining her memories and questioning them. 'We were peasants. I told you. We were brought up to curtsey to the gentry, respect authority and never, never question your role in the scheme of things. Not that they ever thought of it like that. You simply accepted what God and the state and society had ordained for you. The most they could hope for my sister Elke and me was that we'd go into service in one of the big houses and marry a footman if we were lucky. Elke did— go into service, that is. But I swore I never would.'

Brand couldn't help smiling.

'You think that's funny,' she said angrily.

'I'm sorry. I was just thinking, you must have been a problem child to parents like that. Country people everywhere in those days could be very set in their ways, in their expectations of life.'

She smiled back, relenting her flash of anger. 'Oh, I *was* a problem child. "She's too wayward," the nuns told them. I suppose they—my parents—cared for me in their way. But Elke was much more their ideal of what an obedient daughter should be. I was a disturbing influence. Uncomfortable to have around. I think they were relieved when one of the nuns recommended me to a wardrobe mistress at the Festival and she took me on as a temporary seamstress.

'I boarded with three other girls in Salzburg and my father washed his hands of me. In those days in Grinzing, Salzburg was the big city and I could only go to the bad. It was a little step, but it was a beginning.' Her eyes glowed, remembering that first small, exhilarating act of rebellion.

'Just being there, working, seeing those people—even from a distance—artists, singers, musicians, actors! It was a whole new world and I wanted to be a part of it, not just sewing a hem or taking tucks in a bodice, but *really* part of it. During my free time I used to sneak into the music workshops, make out I was a student, spend hours over a cup of coffee in the cafés where the young musicians and singers met. After the season I stayed on. I got a job with a high class dressmaker in the town. I was better than the other girls. Sometimes she let me model her dresses for her customers and I felt wonderfully superior because I knew they could never look as fine in the clothes as I did.

'It was a good time for me, but a bad time, too. Hitler was in power across the border in Germany and he had many Austrian sympathizers. Not that I knew what that meant, or cared. I didn't know anything about politics then, but you couldn't escape the feeling in the air. The Jews were beginning to leave. It was easy for artists. They could continue their careers anywhere—France, England, America. Especially America, that was the Mecca. I wasn't a Jew, the Nazis wouldn't bother me. But there was so much talk of America and I knew I had to get there somehow.'

'And you managed it, you got a job, a sponsor?' said Brand.

She laughed sourly. 'I got a husband. Melvin. Melvin Beasley. God, I barely remember his name. Isn't that dreadful? He was a nice, clean-cut American boy from Phoenix, Arizona. A music student. He'd come to worship at the shrine of Mozart. Instead he got me. It wasn't a fair exchange.'

Again she appeared to be questioning her motives all that time ago. 'I met him at one of the music seminars during the Festival. I was seventeen then and I made him fall in love with me.'

She glanced at Brand through half-lidded eyes, testing him. 'I could, you know, in those days. I was pretty then.'

Watching her, Brand didn't doubt it and said so.

'You don't approve, do you?' she said. 'It wasn't very admirable, not what a nice girl would do. Well, I wasn't

a cutter's assistant. You know, snip, snip, faces on the cutting-room floor. I was bright, eager to learn and—' she chose the phrase delicately—'put myself about. That's how I knew Jake Schneider's father. He was an immigrant too, but long before the Nazis. He was a pig, but important, the way some people in Hollywood can make themselves seem important without actually contributing anything to the creative side of movie-making. Vice president in charge of nothing at the studio. But it was expedient to be nice to him —if you wanted to get on. And I did.'

'Is that why you dislike his son, because of his father?'

'Not entirely. Jake had the sense to adapt to the changing times when the studio system collapsed. But he's just as much of a heel. Underneath. A wheeler-dealer. He gives the impression of being a working producer, always on the set, meddling in everyone's job. That's why he likes working with green directors like Barry. But the only real talent he has is in conning quite sensible business men and film executives into putting up money for his lousy projects. He puts on a good show in the board room and over expense account lunches. But whoever are the losers, it's never Jake. He gets away with it time and again. Maybe he'll get lucky with this movie. But it's a big maybe. He has less feel for what the public will buy than Harry Bass had in his little finger.'

'Who was Harry Bass?' Brand, as an avid filmgoer, knew the name, but he wanted to hear what it meant to Ella Armstrong.

Again, her eyes misted over as they had when she'd spoken of Reinhardt. 'He was my mentor. I think that's the polite term. He was a big producer in those days, epic stuff. Practically every movie he made was nominated for an Oscar and he won quite a few. I met him on the lot at M-G-M. Or, rather, I engineered a meeting. Everyone wanted to work for Harry. But I was clever at making people notice me. At first it was just sex. I expected that. But then he realized I had a genuine gift for organization, for what works and what doesn't on the screen. More and more he asked me to study scripts, give my opinion, long after the affair petered out. Eventually he took me on as a kind of assistant, a glorified personal secretary. He was the best, and I suppose I measure all producers against him. In the early 1950s Britain was opening up its film production and he went over to produce a movie in London. Naturally he took me along. Funny, it was his one misjudgement, his one big flop.'

'And that's when you met Matthew?'

She looked down at her wedding-ring, a plain, insignificant gold band, as if she hadn't seen it for a long time. '*That's* when I met Matthew. He was a raw young actor just starting, but people were saying he had potential. You've no idea how incredibly handsome he was. He was just twenty. I was ten, eleven years older and I'd been around. And I did the damn-fool thing. I fell in love with him. I didn't care that he could never love me. I should have known what I was in for.'

She was silent for a moment, examining her last remark as if, over the distance of time, it would yield an answer for which she'd been searching. If it did, she gave no clue.

'Matthew liked to be seen with an older woman, especially one in such an influential position. It wasn't so strange. And I was pretty ruthless. I'd learned to be. I'm not proud of it. But I still think I was the best thing that could have happened to Matthew. I could see his future, his career, drifting, decent roles but never the lead. Matthew had no drive. He coasted along on his good looks. He needed someone to goad him. And that was me. I thought I could cope with the rest.'

Her knuckles were white as she kneaded the wedding-ring that had suddenly become an irritation. 'You think I'm being disloyal, don't you, Brand? You don't need to say it, I can see it in your eyes. But he *did* need me, not the others.

We were married in a registry office. Harry Bass was there.
He told me I was a fool and I'd be back in a year. But I
stuck it out. I stuck through the bad years when people were
saying, "Matthew Armstrong, he'll never make it." I stuck
through the dreary times when he toured in mediocre plays
and played fathers of the bride in silly British comedies.
And I knew behind his back his *friends* were saying, "How
can he put up with that awful woman?" But I knew why
and in a strange way I think Matthew did. When he did get
that break on Television in *Braddock,* I thought it would
make up for everything. In a way, it did.'

'You never had children?'

'Grow up, Brand' she laughed bitterly. 'People like Matthew and me don't have children. We're each other's children. Besides, Matthew's not. . .' She stiffened warily. 'No,
Brand, that's one shady corner of our life I'll keep to myself.
He was nice, good-natured, easygoing Matthew, never any
trouble to anyone. I was the whipping boy and that was all
right. I never craved affection like he did. I made the difficult
demands for him, I made the unpopular decisions. I had
the arguments with directors and script-writers, the rows
with the agents and producers. "Poor old Matt, what keeps
them together?" they said. What kept us together, Brand,
was survival.

'I didn't mind not being liked. That was part of the deal,
the role I'd elected to play. Except . . . except for Lotte
Bruckner. I wanted her to like me. Why?' She was asking
the question of herself and, from this self-assured woman,
it came out oddly, like the lament of a lonely child who had
been rejected.

'What about Lotte Bruckner?'

She glanced up at him quickly, her face now blank,
uncommunicative. 'Nothing. Nothing at all.'

'Come along now, you two. Mustn't keep the coach
waiting.'

Blanche's friend was passing on the other side of the

street, a breathless Blanche bringing up the rear. The rest of the floral society were nowhere in sight.

'Yes indeed, we mustn't keep the coach waiting, must we, Brand?' She insisted on paying the bill, taking some cruel pleasúre in overriding Brand's protest that she was his guest.

'Well, Brand, this was my life,' she said as she counted out the notes. The lapse into the past tense had the finality of a death wish. 'Do I get charged or let off with a caution? Innocent or guilty? I hope you enjoyed your lunch.'

The look she directed at him was one of unconcealed hatred, the irrational hatred a patient sometimes feels for the psychiatrist who had been reponsible for peeling off the painful layers of a buried past.

CHAPTER 7

On the return trip to Salzburg she ignored Brand, affecting a lively interest in the future plans of the ladies of the floral society who were leaving the next day, although there was some confusion as to where they were going. Blanche insisted it was Munich until it was pointed out that Munich was two days ago. Unrepentant, Blanche confided that all Europe looked pretty much alike to her and on the whole she'd rather be at home in Sacramento.

When the coach deposited Ella and Brand at the Maria-hof, she waved them goodbye gaily and even bought a tape of the film music 'as a memento'. Without glancing at Brand, she walked briskly into the hotel lobby. It was cool and quiet in that late afternoon limbo between lunch and dinner. The tourists were still out exploring the city, the film unit hadn't yet returned.

She was about to leave Brand without a word. He wasn't disconcerted. He understood what it must have cost her to talk so freely about herself. But he couldn't let her go like this. Whatever had troubled her when she first confided in him was still troubling her. Of that, he was certain.

'Ella, if anything worries you, if you feel—well, threatened—you know you can call on me. I'm on the same floor as you and Matthew. The next room, I think.'

She looked pointedly at the hand he'd cupped round her elbow and shrugged it off.

'Oh, that! My dear man, you're not taking seriously that silly little outburst of mine, are you? I can't think what came over me.' Although her manner was skittish, her tone was implacable and he knew she was already regretting revealing so much of herself to him. There would be no budging her in this frame of mind. Better to let it rest. Later, she'd come round.

'It's been a lovely day' she said, dismissing the episode and him with it. The corners of her mouth lifted perfunctorially. Her eyes, refusing to meet his, were scanning the lobby until they focused on something over his shoulder. The smile froze into the same expression of bewilderment and hurt— mostly bewilderment—he'd seen on her face in the summer-house the day before with Lotte Bruckner.

Then she turned on her heel and hurried to the lift.

Brand looked round quickly, wondering what had caused her sudden reaction. But there was nothing to explain it that he could see. Just the reception desk where the impassive Fritz was explaining a railway timetable to a tall, fair, youngish man, presumably a hotel guest, intent on the intricacies of the train schedule.

It was just one more bothering incident to add to all the others.

After her abrupt departure, he'd gone for a walk. But the air was sultry and stale with the promise of another Alpine thunderstorm. Returning to his room, he'd felt the need of a stiff whisky despite the early hour and had taken it into the bathroom attached to his room. He examined his face in the mirror and ran his hand over his chin. He felt years older than he had that morning and was surprised that it didn't show. Other people's confidences placed a heavy toll on the recipient. And the trouble with Brand, as Waller had pointed out more than once, was that he invited them.

From the adjoining bathroom of the next room, he heard the rush of water and above it the opening chorus of *The Sound of Music,* supposedly from a tape-recorder.

Then the clear, soprano voice of Julie Andrews was joined by another, less true and oddly joyless as if the singer were experiencing a deep sadness. The splashing water stopped. Brand felt uncomfortable, being so close to Ella, as if he were yet again invading her privacy.

He picked up his glass and was about to leave the bathroom when his ears caught a faint cry, more unnerving than a scream. 'Oh my God! Brand!' Then, even fainter: '*Warum* . . . ?' Why? And a bump, perhaps a fall.

For a moment after all he could hear was the tape playing out its familiar melodies, sounding almost reassuring. And the rush of water started again as the tap was turned on.

He pounded on the flimsy wall between the two bathrooms. 'Ella!' But there was no reply. Just the music and the water joined in what seemed to Brand an unholy harmony.

For an instant he wondered if he'd imagined that cry. But even as he wondered he hastily pulled on his jacket and made for the door. He was prepared to risk her patronizing smile if it had been nothing, an idle curse uttered to herself in the bath.

The corridor was empty although he could hear the clatter of a typewriter from the production office down the hall. His knock on her door went unanswered. That could be explained if she were in the bathroom, he tried to tell himself. But he knew he didn't mean it. With increasing alarm he banged more loudly on the door, calling her name repeatedly.

He realized the carpet was damp under his feet and he

thought he heard footsteps on the marble stairs round the corner. He paced the corridor in three hurried strides but there was no one there.

'What's going on?' Debbie Price poked her head round the production office door. 'What's all the rumpus? Oh, it's you,' she said when she saw Brand.

'I don't know, but get Fritz the porter—with a key to the Armstrong's room.'

'Why?'

'Don't argue. Get him. Quick.'

She stared at him doubtfully, but responded to the note of authority.

It seemed an eternity before the head porter in his black linen jacket rounded the corridor with a bunch of keys in his hand.

'Open it up,' Brand commanded.

'Really, Herr Brand. I can't just . . .'

'Open it up, man. *Now*.'

Debbie Price and the head porter exchanged dubious looks, but there was no denying the urgency in Brand's voice.

The door opened on to the pleasant, commodious room shared by the Armstrongs, an excuse for a small sitting-room led off to the right. Ella's clothes were neatly folded on one of the twin beds. Everything seemed in order, except for a tracing of damp imprints darkening the carpet which might have been made by anyone padding across the floor with wet feet.

Fritz raised his eyebrows. 'I don't think . . .'

'Not here, you fool, the bathroom—next to mine.'

It was there they found her, lying face up in the deep bath. Her eyes stared blindly up at him. They had the same puzzled expression he'd seen in them when they parted in the lobby., The tap above her was still gushing water and the tiled floor was wet and slippery.

'Christ! She's dead!' Debbie Price stood transfixed at the

sight of that tiny figure with those staring, uncomprehending eyes.

I've failed her, thought Brand numbly, she asked for help and I failed her. Then he realized that Fritz had turned off the tap and was plunging his white-gloved hands into the bath attempting to lift the body. 'She must have slipped. A terrible accident.'

Brand pulled himself together. It wasn't the time for personal recriminations. 'Don't touch anything, Fritz. Leave everything just as it is and call the police.'

After his initial shock, the head porter looked aggrieved as if the corpse constituted a slur on the hotel. 'I could call the local doctor. And I must find the manager. Nothing like this has ever happened before at the Mariahof.'

Damn the hotel, thought Brand. 'Get who you want. But call the police first. Don't worry, Fritz,' he relented, as he saw the man's stricken face. 'It must be reported. I was a policeman in England.'

The bluff, portly sergeant, who painstakingly took their statements in unfamiliar English, was duly sympathetic, but not unduly suspicious. These things weren't unheard of, older people slipping on glazed baths and injuring themselves. Death unfortunately was an inconvenience, involving a lot of paperwork. The husband, of course, would have to be informed. That, from his experience, wouldn't be pleasant either.

The doctor made a cursory examination of the body and then called for an ambulance. Another policeman took notes, asked questions and prowled around the room and bathroom. The hotel manager, interrupted in the middle of an early dinner, was wringing his hands, more concerned about the hotel's reputation than the dead woman.

Brand wished Kiesler were there, but when he suggested it he was politely shown the door along with Debbie Price and the head porter. Kiesler, it appeared, was otherwise engaged. The Salzburg police had more pressing priorities than an elderly lady's 'regrettable accident' in her bathroom. 'We'll call you if we need you,' they were told. Clearly it had occurred to no one but Brand that they might be dealing with something more than a regrettable accident.

And when he'd explained about the cry he'd heard through the bathroom wall, even to Brand it sounded like nothing more menacing than the alarm of a woman who was losing her footing and couldn't save herself. Her unaccountable lapse into German, too—*warum?*—didn't seem peculiar. After all, it was her native tongue. The footsteps on the stairs? He'd only thought he'd heard them, hadn't he? And no one was there anyway. In the sergeant's place, Brand realized, he'd probably have been just as sceptical. But there was something else that nagged at him, something he couldn't put his finger on. A detail, in other circumstances of no consequence. But it was no good trying to force recall. It would come to him eventually, like an elusive name on the tip of the tongue.

By the time the police had finished with Brand and Debbie the film unit had returned from the location. Most of them appeared to have congregated like homing pigeons in the production office of *The Sound of Murder*, perched on chairs and desks, taking in the news of Ella Armstrong's death in their own particular ways, trying to compose a suitable attitude to a tragedy which, to some of them, didn't seem all that tragic. Ella's nuisance value had to a lesser or greater extent permeated the whole production.

'Well, at least its not Matt. I mean . . . if it had been, bang goes the movie,' someone volunteered nervously, echoing the general feeling.

'It's not funny,' snapped Debbie Price. 'You should have seen her. Clear out, all of you. I'll have to contact Jake and Barry. They're not back yet. And Matthew!'

She looked up suddenly at Brand. 'Oh Lord, Matthew!' As members of the unit mooched off in search of a bar and liquid solace, she picked up the telephone, stared helplessly at it for a moment and then put it down. 'I've got to get hold of Matthew.'

'Wasn't he on the location today?' said Brand. Surely that had been the reason why he'd asked Brand to take Ella off his hands, so that she shouldn't be around during his scenes with Lotte Bruckner.

'No. He was supposed to be. But the schedule was re-arranged yesterday.'

'How did that happen?' Since the discovery of Ella's body he'd felt dull and useless, but now his brain was alert.

'You don't have to shout.'

He hadn't realized he'd barked out his question and carefully modulated his voice. 'I'm sorry. But it may be important.'

'You don't think . . .'

'I don't think anything. Just tell me.'

'Lotte was nervous, her first appearance in front of the cameras for ages. We all knew that. She started to rehearse, then she said she wasn't feeling too well, but that she'd be fine when she'd calmed down. So Barry and Jake decided to postpone her scenes with Matt for a couple of days until she'd got a hold of herself.'

'Isn't that unusual?'

'It's not usual. But it happens. Some artists have to be handled with kid gloves and apparently Jake thinks Lotte is one of them. If the timing had been difficult he'd have insisted she go ahead. But we had to reshoot the scenes at the villa between Judy and the blackmailer, after Arthur's heart attack, with—thingummy—Jeremy Fox. So we could easily slot them in with the minimum of disruption. Judy and Jeremy were on call, Matt was on standby where we could reach him if necessary. But it wasn't necessary.'

'Where would you have reached him?'

'Here. Or if he'd gone out he'd have left a number where he could be contacted.'

'When was this decision taken?'

Debbie threw up her hands. 'I don't know. I wasn't there. I was just told.'

'At the lunch-break.' Brand hadn't been aware that the girl named Fred who'd been looking after the journalists had stayed behind in the office after the others had left. She was sitting quietly in the corner thumbing through sheets of contacts of stills photographs.

Brand turned towards her. 'You're certain.'

'Too right. My journalists were very put out. No Matt. No Lotte. And the company wouldn't stake them for another couple of days' stay. They had to make do with Judy who'll do anything for a double-page spread and a couple of photographs. *She's* no problem.'

'Did Ella know about the change of plans?' said Brand, digesting the fact that Matthew had known perfectly well he wouldn't be on call on the day he'd suggested Ella show Brand the sights of Salzburg.

'How should I know?' sniffed Debbie. 'I'm not privy to what he told his wife.'

'And you didn't see him in the hotel at all today?'

Debbie was about to protest that she had other things to worry about than Matthew Armstrong's whereabouts when Fred looked up from her contact sheets. 'You probably wouldn't have found him here. When I took those two journalists out to the airport this morning I saw him in the arrival lounge. I think he spotted me but didn't want to be seen, so he carefully sauntered off in the opposite direction.'

She didn't seem to realize that she'd dropped a small bombshell until she caught the look of surprise that passed between Debbie and Brand.

Debbie's reaction was practical and professional. 'He should have informed me—or someone,' she grumbled.

Brand's was more far-reaching. 'Was he meeting someone?'

'I imagine so. You don't as a rule take a trip to an airport just for the hell of it.'

'Fred's our unit publicist, Mr Brand. Not much misses her, as you may have noticed.' Debbie effected a preoccupied introduction. 'Frederica Hubble. Fred for short. Mr Brand.' Already her mind was racing ahead to the hundred and one things she had to do and Matthew's movements were low on that list of priorities.

'I don't suppose there was anything sinister about it. We all know Matthew,' Fred began to say, then stopped at a warning glance from Debbie and changed the subject. 'Funny old trout. I'll miss her. Ella. I really will. There were times when you wanted to throttle her. But, somehow, I liked her.'

'Funny old trout! Is that how you saw her?' Brand had a mental image of that lively woman of many moods, defying her years, unburdening her life to him so few hours before. Well, at least she'd shed that burden—or someone had shed it for her.

'Strictly a term of endearment, Mr Brand,' Fred explained. 'I've a much juicier vocabulary for the ones I can't stand.'

Brand smiled. Perhaps even Ella wouldn't have minded being described as a 'funny old trout' by this engagingly frank girl.

'I *do* have a lot to do, Mr Brand,' said Debbie Price pointedly.

Brand roused himself from his sad contemplation of the living and now dead Ella. 'Just one more thing.'

'You *did* say you'd been a policeman,' she sighed.

He nodded apologetically. People always tightened up in the presence of the law, even at one remove, like Brand. 'Neither Matthew nor Lotte Bruckner were out on the location. Who else would have been in and out of the production office today?'

'At various times, lots of people. Murray Pick, the location manager. You met him. Jake, Not Barry, he was out early. Fred, of course. The stills man, I think. The production manager. Associate producer. The production office is the heart of the film on location. I know that sounds a bit grand, but it's true. And I can tell you you get bloody fed up when you're stuck here all day looking after everybody's queries —and then this!' 'This,' Brand understood, was the last straw. 'I wonder if the police have managed to get hold of Matt.'

'I'll try and find out,' Brand assured her.

'That would be a relief,' she said gratefully.

As it happened, though, Brand had no need to bother the police. The police were anxious to bother him. His telephone was ringing when he reached his room. It was Kiesler.

'I understand you've managed to find yourself a mystery on your second day in Salzburg,' he said, but if the comment was jovial his tone was serious.

'Mystery?' Brand assumed a surprise he didn't feel.

'The lady in the bath. I gather from my sergeant you suspect it wasn't just an accident. I don't suppose you've any facts to support that?'

'Not what you'd call evidence,' Brand admitted.

'I thought not. All the same, I'd like to hear your story for myself. I'll send a car for you. If you can spare the time. And Ralph,' he added testily, 'do me a favour, keep it to yourself until we've spoken. There's enough genuine crime around to deal with without inventing more.'

CHAPTER 8

Unlike the functional red brick buildings in which Brand had spent most of his working life, the Salzburg City police station on the Domplatz blended unobtrusively with the mellow architecture of the inner city, barely distinguishable from the graceful, time-weathered small hotels and res- taurants that clustered round the tourist centre. But Leo

Kiesler's office, with its businesslike furniture, cluttered 'in' and 'out' trays and insistent telephones, was only too familiar. Brand felt he could have been back behind his old desk in Sussex, except that the coffee he was instantly offered was better. Wherever it was practised in democratic societies, police work was much the same.

The portly sergeant, Schultz, who had taken his statement ushered Brand in. There was a new, slightly aggrieved respect in his eyes. Probably he should have paid more attention to this leathery, large-boned old Englishman and his information, but how was he to know his claim on Inspector Kiesler's friendship was genuine?

Kiesler motioned him to take a seat while he finished a telephone conversation in German too rapid for Brand to catch more than the gist of it, but he gathered it had to do with Ella Armstrong or what remained of her.

'We've managed to locate the husband finally,' said Kiesler, reverting to English as he put down the receiver. 'Glad you could come round so quickly, Ralph.' He didn't sound all that welcoming.

'No trouble,' Brand assured him, dispensing quickly with the courtesies. 'Where did you find him?'

'One of our men spotted him drinking in a bar in the Mozartplatz with a friend. He hadn't been out on the film location and no one seemed to know where he could be. He's made a formal identification of the body.'

'How did he take it?'

'Badly. He broke down.'

'Say anything?'

'Much what you'd expect. He blamed himself for not being with her. The sort of irrational things people say in these—situations.' He chose the word delicately. 'He was too upset to make much sense.'

'Were you able to find out what he'd been doing all day?'

'Not really. He said he'd spent most of it touring in

and around Salzburg. We can check on that later if it's necessary.'

'He didn't mention that he'd been out to the airport.'

Kiesler looked up sharply. 'That he didn't. Meeting someone? Seeing someone off?'

Brand shook his head. 'I only know that the unit publicist on the film was out at the airport and saw him.'

'Well, that's something else.' He sat back in his chair, fixing Brand with a penetrating stare. 'I've just had the doctor's report. Admittedly there hasn't been time for a thorough post mortem. But frankly, Ralph, there's nothing to indicate that it wasn't a straightforward accident. The actual cause of death was almost certainly a fractured skull probably sustained when she slipped in the bath and fell back against the taps. Death was instantaneous. No sign of a struggle.'

'There wouldn't necessarily have been any signs of a struggle if she'd been taken by surprise. After all, she was a small woman, elderly.'

'Granted. But you have to go on the facts. And there aren't any.'

'What about the damp patch I noticed on the carpet in the corridor outside her room when I knocked on the door? The bathroom floor was awash. If there were a killer he'd certainly have got the soles of his shoes wet and left a damp imprint as he slipped out of the room.'

'The waiter spilt a jug of hot water when he delivered the breakfast tray in the morning.'

Brand looked at Kiesler admiringly. 'You don't waste time, do you?'

'We're not quite the sleepy little force we may appear. We just keep a low profile for the tourists' benefit.' Kiesler permitted himself a wry smile. 'But you do see, Ralph, we've absolutely no hard evidence to warrant a murder investigation. Of course there's always a question-mark attached to a sudden death. I know that as well as you do.

And we'll make the usual inquiries. But unless you can furnish me with a sound reason for taking it further, sufficient to satisfy my superior, my hands are tied.'

'Mine aren't,' Brand said quietly.

'If it were anyone else, Ralph . . .' Kiesler sighed. 'All right, tell me what you know about her.'

Sergeant Schultz topped up his coffee as Brand related the events of the day, reliving *The Sound of Music* excursion and Ella's reflections on her life, her unaccountable fear. He edited it all down as succinctly as possible without omitting any relevant information. As he did so his own sense of guilt returned.

When he'd finished Kiesler took a deep breath, letting it out slowly through clenched teeth.

'Not a greatly loved lady, it seems. Interesting. But hardly conclusive, Ralph. In a long lifetime everyone collects a few enemies, but very seldom do they resort to murder.'

'But how do you explain this fear she had that she was being watched?'

'The imaginings of a neurotic woman, perhaps.' Kiesler shrugged. 'After all, Salzburg must have had a lot of distant memories for her and it's the first time she'd returned since she was a girl. She doesn't sound all that stable.'

'Did I give that impression of her?' Brand was surprised. 'She wasn't at all like that. One thing I am sure of was that she was scared. She covered it up well, she was a proud woman. But when she spoke about that feeling of being frightened it was real enough and the hell of it is I'm damned certain she didn't know why. I'm sure it had something to do with her past, long before she became involved in the film business, right here in Salzburg. Maybe it's a blind alley, but that's where all investigations start.'

Kiesler frowned. 'I've too much regard for you, Ralph, to dismiss what you've told me. I know the way you work. You must have a reason for your concern. But on such flimsy suspicions I can't . . .'

'You can do one thing.'

'We'll see,' said Kiesler cautiously.

'Could you find out anything about her early life? Grinzing, I think—that's the village where she was born. She said she's no family there any more. But someone must have remembered her. A priest maybe. The nuns. Neighbours. She worked as a seamstress in Salzburg. I know it's fifty years ago, but there have to be some survivors.'

Kiesler rubbed his chin, considering the request before arriving at a decision. 'That's reasonable. We can make some inquiries. As you say, it's fifty years ago and a lot of records were lost or destroyed during the war. But I'll do what I can.'

'Do you mind if I poke about a bit myself? I won't be encroaching on your patch.'

'Provided I can count on your discretion. I don't want to set off unnecessary alarms. If there's the remotest chance that you may be right—which I doubt—we don't want everyone running scared that they're under suspicion. At the moment it appears we've got an accident, pure and simple.'

His expression softened. 'You really feel deeply about this, don't you, Ralph?'

Brand examined the question and its implications. Kiesler couldn't know just how deeply he felt about it. Prickly and even cruel in her attitude to him, she'd nevertheless offered him her life and he'd been powerless to save it. But there was no way of explaining that to his old friend. 'Once a detective, always a detective,' he said lightly.

Kiesler studied him for a moment, putting his own interpretation on that easy reply. 'Just so long as you remember you've no jurisdiction here.'

'You forget, Leo, I've no jurisdiction in my own country any longer. Just a meddlesome member of the public. I take it you've no objection if I take a look over the Armstrongs' room at the hotel?'

Kiesler pursed his lips. 'I don't see why not. Although I don't know what you expect to find there. We've been over it. The hotel's locked it for the time being. They've given Armstrong another room. I'll put in a call to the manager.'

'Thanks, Leo.' Brand eased himself out of his chair, aware that his bones were aching and he wasn't as young as he used to be.

'Sort of a busman's holiday for you, as they say in England.'

'Sort of. You know where you can find me. Give my regards to Maria.'

'I'll do that.' Kiesler shook his head as he clasped his friend's hand. 'You just can't let it alone, can you, Ralph?'

Brand sank gratefully into the back seat of the car that was waiting to drive him back to the hotel. He wanted nothing more than to surrender to a warm bed and sleep. But he knew he couldn't. Kiesler had been right. He couldn't let it alone. He owed that much to the dead woman.

The hotel manager was waiting for him on his return to the Mariahof. A fussy little man with an exaggerated sense of secrecy, he led Brand to the Armstrongs' room as if they were joint conspirators.

'You'll return the key to me as soon as you've finished, Herr Brand,' he whispered, although no one was around to overhear.

Brand switched on the lights and stood for a moment in the centre of the room. Already it had the anonymous air of transitory occupation. Ella's clothes were just as she'd left them on the made-up twin bed, but they seemed no longer to belong to her. Half the wardrobe was empty. Apparently Matthew had packed a bag for the night when he'd transferred to another room. Even her cosmetics and the paraphernalia of a woman's toilette on the dressing-table appeared ownerless, with no more personality than objects for sale on a chemist's counter. A whiff of *Arpège* assailed his nostrils from an open perfume bottle. But it was just *Arpège* removed from the human flesh that had given it its individual fragrance.

The body in the bathtub had been a case. It was here among her things that Ella seemed truly dead.

He prowled around the room, not sure what he was looking for or even why he was there, opening drawers, cupboards. The lock on the balcony door looked formidable but it had become faulty with age. It gave way under minimal pressure. Brand stepped out on to the small area outside which ran along the length of the hotel floor, each room divided only by a low rail. He supposed that security hadn't been—or had never needed to be—a top priority in the pleasantly old-fashioned Mariahof. He made a mental note to mention that to Kiesler in the morning, although he doubted whether any alert police officer would have missed it.

He leaned his hands on the railings, looking down on a small square below; couples arm-in-arm sauntered across the wet cobblestones, laughing, talking. A sudden shower had cleared the atmosphere. It was after ten, but for the tourists the night was still young. That morning Brand had been one of them, but not any more. A busman's holiday, indeed.

He roused himself from his lazy contemplation of the scene beneath him, realizing that he couldn't delay any longer inspecting the bathroom. For obvious reasons he dreaded it. But it, too, seemed now as impersonal as the bedroom.

But just as he was about to leave his eye caught a glint of something shiny in the crevice between the tiled floor and the wall behind the washbasin. It was trapped in the glare from the bright strip light. By daylight it could easily have been missed.

He bent down and prised it out of its hiding place with his pocket knife, depositing it in his handkerchief, careful not to smudge any possible finger prints. It was a thin, probably gold ballpoint pen, expensive-looking, no ordinary stationer's pen. The breast pocket attachment was loose, well worn. At a guess Brand judged it could have fallen out of someone's pocket without their realizing it. A busy maid might not have noticed it and it could have belonged to a long-gone guest or even one of the Armstrongs. On the other hand, its owner could equally have been the intruder in Ella's bathroom earlier that day.

Brand folded it in his handkerchief and placed it in the inside pocket of his jacket. It was sufficiently individual to be identified without too much trouble and whoever had lost it would certainly want it back. It wasn't much but, Brand suspected, it was the only likely clue that had yet come to light.

It was too late now to bother Kiesler. He'd take it round to him first thing in the morning.

After he'd locked up and returned the key to the manager, Brand looked longingly at his own room next door with its prospect of bed and sleep, then dismissed the thought reluctantly and took the lift to the lobby. Fritz, he'd noticed, was still on duty—was he ever 'off'?—and in this peaceful shank of the evening he'd probably have more time to answer the questions Brand needed to ask.

The head porter let out an imperceptible sigh when Brand approached the desk. But he adjusted his linen cuffs and smiled his formal smile politely.

'Is there anything I can do for you, Herr Brand?'

'Just some information, Fritz,' said Brand, electing not to notice the man's pained expression when his Christian name was used.

'I gave all the information I had to the police—about that unfortunate accident.'

He was going to be difficult, courteous but difficult. Brand couldn't blame him. It had been a hard day for all of them.

He waved his hand airily. 'No, no, not about the accident. Just curiosity. I was wondering about the keys to the rooms.

For my own interest. How many keys are there?'

A flicker of amusement passed over the head porter's face. I'm not fooling him, thought Brand.

'The guests have a key, sir. And we have another. That's all.'

'So both Mr and Mrs Armstrong would have had keys?'

'Of course, sir. But no one else.'

'On the other hand, I suppose some guests leave their doors unlocked when they go out for the day.'

Fritz gave him a pained look. 'That does happen, sir. We strongly advise against it. This is an old hotel and we don't have self-locking fixtures that lock automatically when the door is shut. The manager is going to have them fitted, but obviously it's a job that can't be done at the height of the tourist season.'

So there were two easy accesses to the Armstrongs' room, Brand mentally noted, one through the main door if it had been carelessly left unlocked and the other through the balcony door.

'Was that all, Herr Brand?'

Brand nodded and made to turn away, then deliberately came back as if a sudden unimportant thought had struck him. 'By the way, I'd like to offer my sympathies to Mr Armstrong. What room is he staying in now?'

'I'll telephone his room, but I don't think he's here.'

'You haven't seen him?'

'Not recently. He came back earlier with a friend and packed a bag.'

'After his wife died?'

'No. Just before you returned from your trip with Mrs Armstrong.' Busying himself with the hotel register, he didn't notice Brand's look of surprise.

'Have you any idea where he went?'

'It's not my business, Herr Brand . . .'

Brand interrupted him abruptly. 'I understand your reluctance to talk about your guests, Fritz. It does you

credit. But I would like to get in touch with him. Inspector
Kiesler . . .'

He dropped the name into the conversation and let it lie
there reproachfully, reminding the head porter that Brand
was no routine guest but an associate of the Inspector.

'Mr Armstrong asked me to book a room in his name at
the Stadt Hotel. It's very small, not far from here.'

'When was this?'

'Yesterday. About lunch-time. He telephoned. Asked me
to recommend a discreet hotel. It's quiet, comfortable, away
from the traffic.'

'You spoke about Mr Armstrong returning today to pack
a bag with a friend. Have you any idea who the friend was?
A member of the film unit?'

The head porter's expression indicated that he'd gone far
enough in betraying the confidence of his calling to satisfy
Brand's curiosity. Even if he was a friend of Inspector
Kiesler.

CHAPTER 9

Despite a detailed study of the street map Brand had some
difficulty finding the Stadt Hotel. It was tucked away from
the main thoroughfares in a modest courtyard lit only by a
single lamp. Like a lover engaged in an illicit liaison, it didn't
advertise itself and the weary porter who was considering
locking up for the night didn't welcome this late visitor too
heartily. (After midnight guests were required to ring the
bell.) He grumpily looked up the hotel register and admitted
that a Herr Armstrong had registered that day. No, he
didn't recall when he'd arrived because he hadn't been on
duty. And no, he wasn't permitted to give Brand his room
number unless he was announced.

In his less than fluent German Brand managed to convey

that the matter was urgent, so would he please announce him.

Grudgingly the man picked up the phone. After a few moments he got a reply and a garbled message was relayed.

He cupped his hand over the mouthpiece. '*Ihr Name, bitte?*'

Brand thought quickly. Armstrong could legitimately refuse to see Brand, but he could hardly turn down the local law. On the other hand, with his imperfect command of the language, by no stretch of the imagination could Brand pass himself off as a native.

He chose his words carefully. '*Ich war hier bei Inspektor Kiesler geschickt.*' It could mean anything and it was only half a lie to suggest that he was Kiesler's messenger. '*Stadt Polizei,*' he added, knowing he was pushing his luck but prepared to risk it. The porter looked dubiously at Brand, but the Inspector's name had the desired effect. He shrugged. It was none of his business.

There was another delay as Armstrong presumably digested the information. Then the porter put down the phone. '*Zimmer sieben. Links.*' He pointed with his left hand to the winding stairway that led off the lobby, his eyes following Brand as he mounted the stairs.

As he tapped on the door it was opened immediately. Brand braced himself for Armstrong's reaction. He was prepared for almost anything, surprise, disbelief, anger, but not for the response he got.

'Oh, it's you Brand.' His tone was resigned, beyond argument. It was as if Armstrong had been expecting him. It was Brand who was shocked. The face in the dimly lit doorway seemed a haggard caricature of the jaunty likeness that had graced the Television screen, the eyes hollow and sunken, the eyelids puffy, the carefully disguised lines of age were now deeply etched into the sagging flesh that hung loosely from his cheekbones. He had been drinking heavily and he looked twenty years older.

'You'd better come in.' He opened the door wider. Even

his body appeared to have shrunk in on itself, his movements no longer springy, but slow and cautious like the actions of an old man fearful of injuring himself. 'I didn't think it would take you so long.' He conjured up the ghost of a smile which for an instant rearranged his face into a semblance of its old handsome image.

'Martin,' he called. 'It's all right. This is a friend of mine. At least—' his eyes pleaded with Brand—'I hope he is.'

Brand was about to reassure him, to offer the usual comfortless condolences, when a tall, blond man probably in his early thirties came out of the bathroom. He leaned his long, lithe body diffidently against the frame of the door, his expression wary.

It was the same man Brand had seen in the lobby of the Mariahof studying the railway timetable with Fritz. The man, he assumed, who had provoked Ella Armstrong's sudden pained bewilderment when they'd returned from the trip. A nightmare ago.

'Well, now you know it all, Brand. What can we offer the inspector? Sorry, former inspector.'

The younger man shook his head almost imperceptibly at Brand: a slight but unmistakable gesture of warning. 'You've had enough, Matt.'

'There isn't enough. Brand?' The drink didn't seem to have impaired his speech. He'd reached the stage when it no longer had any effect, until hopefully he simply passed out.

'No, thanks,' said Brand. 'Empty stomach.'

Armstrong's companion shot a grateful look at him.

'I'm forgetting my manners. Martin Elliott. Ralph Brand.' Armstrong waved his hand from one to the other as if it didn't belong to him.

The actor slumped into an armchair and for a moment seemed to have lost track of where he was. Watching him, this sad, sodden wreck of a man drenching whatever grief he was experiencing with alcohol, Brand felt guilty. He'd forced himself on Armstrong when the actor was especially vulnerable and, faced with the consequences, he knew he had no right to be there.

Whatever Armstrong told him tonight in his present frame of mind he'd regret it bitterly tomorrow. And what more indeed could he tell him? The presence of Martin Elliott said it all—or most of it. If he questioned him now at his most defenceless, he wondered whether his conscience wouldn't allow him to betray that confidence. He had always lacked that necessary attribute of the ruthlessly competent detective—objectivity. Witnessing distress, he felt impelled to share it.

'I'm sorry, I shouldn't have come. It'll keep till tomorrow.'

'Ah, but it won't, Brand. I'm glad you did come.' Armstrong's shrunken body rocked gently backwards and forwards in the armchair, his bloodshot eyes unseeing but curiously absorbed, as if his life were being re-run across the retina like some old dated movie. 'I didn't kill her,' he said suddenly.

'Matt, for God's sake, stop it!' It wasn't said out of fear. There was a genuine concern in Martin Elliott's voice. 'Mr Brand, you can see . . .'

'No, Martin. What's the use? It'll all come out anyway. Somehow.' Armstrong sounded more lucid now as if his few moments of reflection had sobered him up.

'What makes you think your wife was killed?' said Brand quietly.

'I don't know. Just—a feeling. Premonition, perhaps. I'm right, aren't I? Your chum. What's his name? Kiesler? He must have put you up to this. Trap him while his defences are down.'

'No. Inspector Kiesler didn't send me,' Brand admitted. 'That wasn't strictly the truth.'

'But near enough. You had to do a neat job of detecting to find me. You wouldn't have gone to all that bother just to offer me your sympathy in my *grief.*' He picked the word out of the air and embellished it with a gruesome chuckle. Then the chuckle turned sour on him. He stared solemnly past Brand at some inner vision that gave him no pleasure. 'The odd thing is, I *am* grieving. We belonged together. Even when we hated each other, which was most of the time, we needed each other too. I love Martin. But I needed her. That's something for you to think about, Brand.'

Martin Elliott placed a comforting hand on his shoulder and Armstrong seized it hungrily. He held it for a moment, then let go. Elliott stood there awkwardly, seemingly unsure how to react to Armstrong's admission of his divided loyalties, although he must have been aware of them. Then he turned aside abruptly.

'I'll see if I can get that old buzzard downstairs to rustle up some black coffee.' On his way to the door he faced Brand. 'You look like a kind man, Mr Brand. Even if you were a policeman. I hope you are.'

'What were you doing at the Mariahof today?' Brand doubted whether the question was kind but it had to be asked.

'I saw you too.' Martin Elliott smiled bleakly. 'I was waiting for Matthew while he packed a bag. I was checking out the times of the trains to Innsbruck and Munich. I know policemen like to have chapter and verse. The porter will bear me out,' he added. His steady blue eyes, not unlike Ella's, stared gravely at Brand. 'If he flakes out before I get back, just cover him with a blanket. I'll look after him. He'll be right as rain tomorrow. He always is.' He sounded as if he were used to it.

'Decent chap. They weren't all decent. But Martin is.'

Brand became aware that Armstrong had been watching them intently. He felt a reply of some sort was required but the actor forestalled him.

'You didn't know I was gay. Well, no reason why you should. It's not something you advertise when you're in the

public's eye.' Brand didn't betray his surprise. He hadn't
suspected the actor was gay. But then why should he? As
he'd said, he hadn't advertised the fact. Then a sudden
thought struck Armstrong and he looked at Brand with
disbelief. 'You don't seriously think I might murder my wife
for fear she'd find out I was homosexual!'

'I don't think anything.'

Armstrong pounded his forehead with his fist as if trying
to force himself to think straight. 'No, that's not right.
Because she was standing in the way of me and Martin.
Maybe that's what's buzzing around in your funny mind.'
He made idle circles with his index finger.

'There've been stranger motives for murder.'

Armstrong's hollow laugh made Brand feel foolish, as it
was intended to do. 'My dear chap, for a man of the world,
you amaze me. This is show business. Everyone in the
business knows I'm gay. Ask anyone on the set from the
chippies upward.'

With a shaking hand he lit a cigarette from the pack on
the table beside him. 'And you can't imagine Ella didn't
know. She knew almost from the first day I met her all those
years ago. In those days before the Wolfenden Report if you
were an actor with a virile image—' he seemed to find that
amusing and repeated it—'a virile image, that's a joke.
What was I saying? Oh yes. If you were like me, the safest
thing was to marry quickly, preferably an older woman who
didn't mind or was prepared to live with it. In those innocent
bygone days the fans believed if you were married you had
to be straight.'

'And was Ella prepared to live with that?'

Armstrong stubbed out the cigarette with a gesture of
distaste. 'Ella wanted to be married to a star and she was
prepared to put up with anything for that. It just took a lot
longer than she'd expected. When I was younger I missed
out. But it happened as she'd planned—eventually. At least
she died married to a star.'

His eyes had begun to glaze over, the effects of the heavy drinking were catching up with him. After the sudden period of alertness he'd be gone, no good to himself or Brand.

'Why did you ask me to keep her occupied today, away from the location, when you knew you wouldn't be on call?'

Armstrong looked up at him shamefaced. 'I landed you, didn't I? Sorry, sorry, old boy. I wasn't lying when I said I modelled Braddock on you,' he added for some irrelevant reason of his own.

'We had a good day.'

'I'm glad. You see—' He heaved himself to the edge of the chair, then slumped back. 'You see, I was waiting for an opportunity for Martin to join me. Didn't want to stir it up. Same old rows. I said she didn't care, but she did. If she knew Martin was coming there'd have been an argument. But once he was here she'd accept it, like she always did.'

'So you phoned him when you heard the schedule was being rearranged and booked a hotel room. That's why you were at the airport this morning, to meet him.'

Armstrong snickered unpleasantly. 'Oh, what a busy little beaver you've been. I should have had better sense. But you were available, old boy. A godsend, you might say. It wasn't only because of Martin. That just happened. Ella was making a nuisance of herself on the set, as she always did. Protecting my interests, she'd say. I just—I just wanted to be free of her for a bit. You can understand that, can't you? And she seemed to take to you. There—that's the truth.'

'When you came back to the hotel to collect a suitcase, did you see her?'

Armstrong squeezed his fingers hard against his temples, trying to remember. 'No, no, I didn't see her. I heard her. You were back early and I was packing the bag. Just a few things. I didn't want to face her. So I stepped out on the balcony. She didn't notice me. Then when she went into the bathroom for something I slipped out.'

'Was anyone around at the time?'

'I don't know. I don't know.' He sounded truculent. 'Why are you asking me all these questions? What are you doing here?' he asked suddenly as if the last half-hour had been blotted out of his mind. 'I didn't invite you. Where's Martin?'

He looked at Brand as if he were a stranger, lunged out of the chair, stood swaying for a second and then fell heavily. Brand grabbed him by the arm to lift him back. As he did so he noticed deep scratches on his wrist, the blood had dried, staining his shirt sleeve.

'Where . . . ?' he began to say, then he realized that Matthew Armstrong had passed into an alcoholic oblivion.

He collected a blanket from the bed and covered the inert body with it, pushing a cushion behind his head. He hadn't noticed that Martin Elliott had returned. He was holding a tray with a pot of coffee and cups.

'You'd think I was asking for the Crown Jewels,' he said, nodding at the sleeping man. 'Wasted effort, I see. I hope you got what you wanted, Mr Brand.'

Brand sighed. 'It was necessary.'

'Necessary? I'm glad you think so. Couldn't you have left him alone? Just tonight.'

'I know what you must think of me. But it doesn't matter. What matters is that his wife is dead and maybe she's been murdered. That's not the official opinion. Just mine. If you care for him you'll realize that he might be in a difficult position. He was at the hotel just before she died. He was having an affair. Doesn't matter whether it was with a man or woman. How did Armstrong get those scratches on his arm?' He slipped in the question suddenly, hoping to catch him off guard.

Meticulously, Elliott poured himself a cup of black coffee and made Brand wait while he drank it. Then finally he said: 'Drunks have an uncanny knack of colliding with sharp objects and not even noticing it. Not that he was an habitual drinker. Just sometimes. When it all got too much. I'll testify to that.'

'Why was he so anxious for Ella not to know you were arriving today?'

Elliott shrugged. 'Probably one of the times when he'd told her the affair was over. He did that periodically and I assume she believed him, until she learned otherwise. We've been together five years. It was better for him than one-night stands. I think she understood that.'

'And you didn't mind?'

Elliott looked across at Armstrong now snoring quietly into the cushion. His expression was fond, resigned. 'You can't mind. Matt is what he is. Weak, dependent. But you love him all the same. Everyone does. It was poor old Ella who took the flak. You know, Brand, whatever you may think, I work hard for a living. I'm an interior decorator. At least, that's what I like to call myself. Actually I'm a self-employed decorator. And this was supposed to be a nice little holiday for me.'

Despite his weariness, Brand mustered a wan smile. 'It was supposed to be a nice little holiday for me, too.'

'It still can be—for you. All you have to do is walk out of this door and forget you ever saw Matt like this—with me. None of the unit will talk. They're a close-mouthed lot to outsiders. And they like Matt.'

'I can't do that.'

'No. I forget. Once a policeman, always a policeman.'

Brand withdrew his handkerchief from his inside jacket pocket and exposed the slim gold pen he'd found in Ella's bathroom.

'Do you recognize this?'

Elliott reached out to pick it up.

'Don't touch it,' Brand warned.

'Ah, evidence! It's expensive, I'd say. But it's not mine.'

Carefully pocketing the pen, Brand realized Elliott hadn't precisely answered his question.

The younger man's expressionless blue eyes gave nothing away and they haunted Brand as he walked heavily down the stairs and into the courtyard outside.

CHAPTER 10

'Brand!'

Hearing his own name piercing through the lobby of the Mariahof, Brand sighed. He recognized the fruity American voice of Jake Schneider and from the sound of it, well lubricated with liquor, its owner was feeling no pain.

'Brand!' the producer hailed him again, just in case he hadn't heard the first time. When Brand reluctantly acknowledged the call, he beckoned him over to the bar. Brand sympathized with the bartender who was smothering a yawn.

'Come and join the wake.'

Schneider's fellow mourner, Fred Hubble, winced.

'Sorry, bad joke.' But there was no apology in the producer's tone.

'It's awfully late, Jake,' the girl protested. 'I've already had the *Sun*, the *Mail*, the *Express* and the *Los Angeles Times* on the phone. They all want exclusive interviews with Matt about his late wife. It's going to be a tough day tomorrow, even supposing Matt's up to it.'

Schneider patted the girl patronizingly on the cheek. 'Calm down, Fred, Matthew will be all right.'

'For Christ's sake, the man's wife is dead!'

'Matthew will be all right,' Schneider repeated less soothingly. 'I know him. Besides, the publicity won't do the film any harm.'

After his encounter with Armstrong Brand doubted whether he'd be all right for anything, let alone the massed legions of the Press. 'I don't think . . .' he began to say, but

Schneider motioned him to take a seat. 'What'll it be? A toast to our dear, departed Ella.'

'Jake!' The girl seemed about to make some irate comment, but she bit back her anger, either from discretion or expedience. After all, for the length of the production Schneider was her employer.

Schneider turned his back on the publicist and leaned across the table, his face uncomfortably close to Brand's. 'Everyone's deserting me. How about a nightcap? And then you can tell me what you don't think.' Like Armstrong, he seemed to have the capacity to sober up when it suited him.

'I don't think Matthew Armstrong will be in any fit condition for much tomorrow,' said Brand. Out of the corner of his eye he saw Schneider and Fred Hubble exchange a silent question.

'I didn't,' said Fred in answer to the producer's unspoken query.

'I found out from the porter where he was staying,' Brand elaborated. 'At least, I put two and two together. I don't suppose it occurred to you to notify the police that he wasn't at the Mariahof, assuming he hadn't himself.'

'The police!' Schneider was fully sober now. 'Why would the police be interested?'

Brand let the man suffer for a few moments. 'I think I will have that drink. Just Perrier and ice.' He realized that his personal dislike to Schneider and his callous reaction to Ella's death were adding to his perverse pleasure in watching him squirm. The Press was one thing, a police investigation quite another. But in all conscience Brand couldn't prolong the suspicion he'd planted in Schneider's mind that the police had reason to suppose Ella's death wasn't an accident. Already he'd exceeded his promise to Kiesler.

'Simply a formality.'

Schneider's relief was visible. 'You mean they don't suspect . . . I mean, there's nothing—funny about it?'

Brand couldn't resist a further dig. 'I don't know, Mr Schneider. It depends what you think is funny.'

'*Touché*,' murmured Fred. 'If you don't mind, I've got about five hours' sleep ahead of me—if I'm lucky.' She turned on her heel without saying goodnight. Schneider didn't seem to notice.

The producer composed his face into an ingratiating mask for Brand's benefit, although the effort was somewhat impaired by his unfortunate squint. 'I'm afraid we're all a bit edgy, Brand. Nasty business.'

'But good for publicity?'

The mask slipped momentarily. 'Well, every little helps. Doesn't matter what they write provided they spell the name of the movie right. We're not really as cold-blooded as we seem.' The plural 'we' seemed misplaced. The cold-bloodedness was all on Schneider's side.

He leaned close to Brand again as if imparting some profound but secret truth. 'You see, we're in the middle of a production. Millions of dollars are at stake. My concern is getting the thing finished. Any little hiccup could foul it up.'

'Like a police inquiry?'

'Don't say that, even in jest.' Schneider shuddered. 'Anyway, that's not even a suggestion. Is it?'

Brand sighed. 'No,' he admitted.

'Well, then. The show goes on.'

'You mean you'll be filming tomorrow?'

'Have to keep to schedule—at least what's left of it.'

'And you really think Armstrong will be able to cope?'

'Don't you worry about Matt. Now that he's got his boyfriend with him, he'll be OK.'

'When did you learn he'd changed hotels? Earlier this evening no one knew where he was. Unless you were all lying.'

Schneider raised his hands in mock humility. 'Matt told me this morning. I didn't spread it around. They'd find out soon enough and he wasn't on call. And who would have cared?'

'Ella maybe.'

'Ella could lump it, as you English say.' There was no mistaking the venom in his voice. Oddly, Schneider seemed unaware how damning it sounded.

'Or was this the one time Ella couldn't lump it any longer?'

Schneider looked at him shrewdly. 'You don't seriously think Matt feels any grief over her death?'

'He said he did and he certainly behaved as if he did. Maybe you don't know him as well as you think.'

'I don't know what sort of a front he put up with you, but he must be thanking his lucky stars he's rid of her. That woman was a plague. True, I didn't get to know him well until we started negotiating this movie. But it didn't take long to realize she'd been buggering up his life for years.'

'And buggering up yours—as you so delicately put it— too, I gather.'

Schneider jerked back, his eyes mean little slits. 'Why do you say that?'

'I understood from Ella—and Matthew, by the way— that if this film takes off you want to make a follow-up. Only this time, Ella insisted, you weren't going to get her husband on the cheap.'

'That's just talk. Listen, feller, every time you set up a movie there's a hassle over money. Suddenly the actor thinks he's a superstar because he got good notices last time and that he should be paid as much as Robert Redford. It's routine.'

'Ella didn't seem to think it was routine. She sounded very determined.'

'Look, Brand, I may not be Mary Poppins, but don't tie me in with Ella's murder.'

'Who said anything about murder?'

Schneider was fighting to control himself, grabbing at

straws. 'You did. A murder investigation, you said.'

'No, I didn't. You just weren't listening, Mr Schneider. I simply said that the police should have been notified where Armstrong was staying tonight.'

'Well, you implied it. What the hell's your interest in this anyway, Brand?'

'Justice.' It was a large word for Schneider to swallow but Brand suddenly realized it summed up exactly his interest in Ella's death.

As he tried to digest Brand's reply, the producer absent-mindedly fingered the fraying threads of a strip of plaster under his chin, until he noticed Brand watching him and abruptly removed his hand from his face like a small boy caught picking a pimple.

'Damned electric shaver cut out. It's a long time since I've had to use a regular razor,' he explained more elaborately than he needed to. Then he switched on that all-purpose smile which lit up as abruptly as a light-bulb, emitting as little warmth.

'Oh boy, this is really heavy. Too heavy for me. You're just kidding, aren't you? What do you call it? Hypothetical? I guess it comes from having been a policeman. Someone dies. Look for a suspect. Everybody dies, Brand. Me? I'm as sorry as anyone that Ella had to die that way—whatever you may think.' The words tumbled out rapidly as if he were improvising a film script on the spot.

'That's right, Mr Schneider. It's all hypothetical,' said Brand heavily.

The producer gave a nervous laugh. 'Well, then!' He made a great display of looking at his watch. 'Is it really that late?'

'It's been that late for quite a while.'

Schneider ignored the remark. 'You know, Brand, I'm really glad you're here.' The suddenly chummy tone rang false and Brand raised a sceptical eyebrow.

'No, honestly I am. It's going to be a sticky day, what

with the Press and everything. Matt'll be grateful for a supportive friend.' Amazing, thought Brand, how everyone assumed that he and Armstrong were bosom buddies. 'I'd appreciate it if you could come out on the set, stick around, help smooth things over for him.'

'You mean you'd like to keep an eye on me? Make sure I don't ask any awkward questions.'

The producer feigned an exaggerated lack of understanding. 'What do you mean by that?'

Brand shook his head. He was tired of bandying words with the man. 'Nothing. You do realize there'll be an inquest of some sort, Matthew will be needed for that. And then arrangements for the funeral. It's all going to take time, and time, I gather, is what you haven't got on this production.'

'Sure, sure, we've got people who can take care of all that. Just so long as the guy's in shape for filming.' Schneider motioned to the bartender and fumbled in his breast pocket as he studied the bill. The man waited patiently, then produced a ballpoint of his own for Schneider's signature.

'So, Brand, I'll see you in the morning,' he said as he scrawled his name across the bill, underlining it with a showy flourish. He sounded as if he'd just concluded a satisfactory business deal.

'Why did Lotte Bruckner order Ella off the set the other day?' Brand had been saving the question. He watched Schneider's reaction with interest. The producer didn't look up, seeming to pay inordinate attention to the signature he'd just written.

'Did she?'

'You know very well she did. It was after that she didn't feel able to continue filming. You had to rearrange the schedule.'

'Oh, that! It was nothing. Just temperament. Some artists don't like strangers around when they're working.'

'It seemed pretty open house to me. I was a stranger. It was Ella she took exception to.'

'Well, if she'd seen you maybe she'd have sent you packing.' He seemed to find that amusing. 'Now, if you'll excuse
me Brand, I'll have to get some shut-eye. I don't usually
keep these sort of hours when we're shooting.'

He flashed another of those cold, practised smiles at
Brand and was off. Leaving Brand feeling he'd taken up
more of the producer's precious time than he was entitled
to and wondering at what point the boozy joker who'd urged
him to 'join the wake' earlier had regretted his impulsive
invitation.

As he lay in his bed next door to the Armstrongs' now
vacant room, Brand stared at the ornate, darkened ceiling.
Sleep eluded him, his busy brain at odds with his weary
limbs. The silence of the night was punctuated by the distant
rumble of traffic, the occasional wail of a police or ambulance
siren. If he had any sense, he'd leave tomorrow, he told
himself. He could travel on to Innsbruck, Vienna. After all,
he bore no responsibility for what had happened the day
before. Kiesler would understand. Kiesler would probably
be only too pleased to be rid of an interfering retired police
inspector who refused to accept facts as fact. There were
limits to friendship.

He turned on his side angrily, bunching the bedclothes
around him. That's what he'd do, leave tomorrow. To hell
with Matthew Armstrong and *The Sound of Murder*. And to
hell with Ella? No, he couldn't quite think that yet. All the
same, she'd been willed on him. He hadn't volunteered.
Why should he alone be bothered about how she met her
death?

He sat up suddenly in bed. For a moment he wasn't quite
sure why. Then he realized it was another noise. Not traffic,
not police sirens, not clicking footsteps on the pavement
below. It was a stealthy sound made by someone anxious
not to be heard. And he could have sworn it came from the
room next door. He strained his ears, but the noise had
stopped. He must have imagined it. But then again he

detected it. A shuffling, groping fumble in the dark. Quietly he got out of bed and moved to the balcony door. The night air was chill and, shivering, he grabbed the jacket he'd draped over a chair and placed it round his pyjama shoulders.

Prising the door open, he stepped out on to the terrace, edged along to the low rail separating the two rooms and carefully stepped across it, wincing as his bare foot made contact with the metal strut at the base of the rail.

At first as he peered through the glass balcony door into the room he could see nothing but the looming shapes of furniture. Then he became aware of a huddled figure moving round the room behind a small beam of light, probably from a torch. There seemed no pattern to its movements. The intruder appeared to be searching for something and Brand was fairly sure what he—or she—must be prepared to take such a risk to find.

There was little chance that he could nudge open the loosely latched door without being heard and it was likely that the searcher was more agile than he. Surprise was his only weapon. Taking several deep breaths, he grasped the door handle and pulled it sharply towards him, hearing the click of the faulty lock as it opened.

The noise caught the trespasser off guard. The torch clattered to the floor, its light shooting a frail beam that fanned out eerily across the carpet. 'What the devil?' It was a man's voice. For a second the figure remained motionless, then it bounded up, making a dash for the main door.

'I wouldn't do that,' said Brand. 'It's locked. You'll wake up the whole hotel. Besides, I know who you are.'

Brand felt along the wall for a light switch and, in the sudden glare, he found himself staring into the face of Murray Pick. The man's eyes swivelled frantically round the room looking for an escape that wasn't there. Then his tense body relaxed into a posture of resignation.

'Is this what you were looking for?' Brand produced the handkerchief enclosing the gold pen from his jacket pocket.

Murray Pick nodded. 'How did you . . . ?'

'Don't worry, the police didn't find it. I did, earlier this evening.' For some unaccountable reason he felt compelled to reassure the man. Unwise, Brand, he thought, unwise. But he doubted whether Pick was up to murder to get it back. 'Maybe we should have a little talk.'

Pick managed to muster a show of truculence. 'I don't have to answer your questions.'

'Mine. Or the police. Take your choice.'

'I guess I don't have any.' The man looked exhausted as if the effort of his furtive search had temporarily drained the spirit out of him.

'Let's go next door. I've a bottle of duty free. You look as if you need it' said Brand as he turned off the light and led Pick to the balcony door. 'I assume you got in the same way as I did. Hadn't you better take that with you?' He nodded at the torch on the carpet.

As Pick bent down to retrieve it he glanced up, seemingly weighing up a possible course of action. Brand had a shrewd idea what was going through his mind.

'I wouldn't risk it if I were you. Too much noise,' he said reasonably.

Pick leant heavily on his hands. 'You've got an answer for everything.'

'Not everything.' Brand shivered. 'Come on. It's cold out here and my feet are killing me.'

After he'd poured tots of whisky into tooth mugs, he studied the man who was crouched in the one comfortable chair in Brand's room. In the car on the way to the film set he'd been remote, efficient and barely polite, just another member of that closed community that comprised a movie crew on location. Only his calculated refusal to acknowledge Ella had singled him out from the rest. Now, caught in a secretive act that Brand suspected was foreign to his nature, he assumed an identity. The face was frank and open and, even in the stress of the moment, he gave off an air of good humour, the kind of man who from years of experience would take the irritations of his job in his stride: probably capable of sudden explosions of temper but quick to forgive and forget. Yet whatever had prompted his actions up to his discovery by Brand in the darkened room next door must have been extraordinarily powerful. The recovery of his gold pen could only have seemed that urgent in the light of a greater urgency.

He'd hardly sipped his whisky, grasping the mug with two strong hands as if it were a lifeline. 'Why don't you just turn me in?' he said finally.

'I'd rather hear from you why you were in Ella Armstrong's room before her death. You were, weren't you?'

'No.' Murray Pick's hollow laugh had no mirth in it. 'That's the joke.'

'But the pen?'

'Oh, I was in her room all right.'

'Why?'

The man raised his eyelids and looked up at Brand without lifting his head. It was a gesture Brand had seen actors use for dramatic effect. But Pick was no actor and the drama was rooted in some nagging secret he could no longer conceal.

'I intended to kill her. And you see, the joke is someone had beat me to it.'

CHAPTER 11

Brand sat down awkwardly on the bed. The simplicity of Murray Pick's confession was more unexpected than the confession itself.

'How do you know someone had got there first?'

Pick looked at Brand quizzically. 'Didn't you hear what I said?'

'I heard.'

'I wanted to kill her. Doesn't that shock you?'

'After forty years in the police force nothing much shocks me,' Brand replied wryly.

'You're a rum bastard.'

'Possibly. But I still want to hear how you know someone got there first.'

'Because as I let myself into her room by the balcony, the main door was just being pulled shut. I heard the click. That and the water running in the bathroom.'

'You didn't see anyone leave the room?'

'No, just the door closing and the click. I went into the bathroom and there she was. Even then it never occurred to me that she might have fallen accidentally. I knew it was no accident. I'll never forget the look on her face.' Pick stared intently ahead of him, conjuring up that image of the dead woman. 'It wasn't horror, but surprise, as if she didn't know why she was being murdered.'

'I know. Go on.'

'I bent down to look at her although I knew she was dead. Then I heard you thumping on the door. I panicked and got out the way I came in.'

'And as you bent down your pen slipped out of your pocket. That's where I found it. In the bathroom.'

Murray Pick nodded. 'It was only afterwards that I noticed I'd lost it. If it were just any old ballpoint it wouldn't have mattered. But this one was special. I knew it could have been traced to me. I looked everywhere for it and then I realized I must have dropped it in her room somewhere —I didn't think of the bathroom straight away—and I had to get it back.'

'It didn't occur to you to go to the police?'

Pick shook his head. 'No. If someone wanted to kill her as badly as I did, they deserved to get away with it' he said bitterly. 'Besides, it was only my word that someone had been in the room before me. I know I'm in a mess now. But you needn't expect any remorse from me. I'm glad it happened.'

'Vengeance, as they say, is sweet—even if someone else does the job for you?' Everything the man had said condemned him, morally if not technically, and Brand wondered why his overriding feeling was one of pity for him.

'Something like that.'

'How could you be so sure that no one would have seen you enter her room?'

'I was supposed to meet Jake in the production office late afternoon. We had to untangle some location problem and I couldn't pin him down on the set. But when I got to the office he wasn't there. It was empty. Debbie had obviously been called away. I hung about a bit and then went out on to the balcony. That's when I saw Ella. Two rooms along. She was on her balcony. She didn't notice me. She was looking down into the street, sort of mesmerized. I almost thought she was going to jump. Then she started humming that infernal song from *The Sound of Music*. And it brought it all back to me. When she went in I stayed on the balcony thinking and remembering. Then I decided. After fifteen years I had finally decided. And I felt a tremendous sense of relief.'

He paused for a moment, then he pulled himself back from that brink of memory buried in the past fifteen years before. 'I didn't know how I was going to do it, only that I would. I heard Debbie return and start typing. She didn't see me outside. So I made my way along to Ella's balcony over those low railings. She'd left the door open and—well, you know the rest. When I got back afterwards, I slipped into the production office while Debbie was in the corridor with you and out through the door and down the stairs when the coast was clear. The coast was clear!' he repeated, attempting a feeble smile. 'Funny, how life mirrors the movies. Reality writ in film clichés.'

Then he buried his head in his hands. His shoulders heaved as he tried to smother the dry, racking sobs he could no longer contain.

Brand remained silent, knowing now why he felt such pity for the man. After a few moments, Pick pulled himself together and stared bleakly at Brand. 'Well, why don't you ask me?' he said finally.

'All right. Why?'

'A murder for a murder.'

'Ella Armstrong committed murder?'

'As good as. He was only a boy. Nineteen. It was during a summer season of *The Sound of Music* that they met. Matthew and Tom. It was a tacky production. Matthew wasn't a star then, but he had enough of a name to pull in the punters. He was playing von Trapp and Tom was the eldest boy of the Trapp family. He was far too old for the part but he always looked so . . . so very young, blond hair, delicate face, almost like a girl's. And he had a good voice. He hadn't any track record as an actor, but he was the sort of boy you noticed on stage. And they only paid peanuts. He was so excited, just to get a half-way decent part. It wasn't long before Matthew became attracted to him. You know he's gay, I suppose? So was Tom. At least, I think he could have gone either way until he met Matthew. It was a real love-affair. It went on all through the run of the show.'

'Did Matthew feel the same way?'

'I think so. As much as he feels anything. And he was good to Tom, good *for* him. He gave him advice, put him in touch with a live-wire agent.'

'And what went wrong?'

'What do you think? Ella! I gather she put the pressure on Matthew to give Tom up. But that wasn't the worst of it. She confronted Tom and made him feel like a home-wrecker. Then she undermined him, destroyed his confidence in his own talent, put it about that he was unreliable, a trouble-maker.'

'How could she do that? Surely she didn't carry that much weight in the profession.'

'She didn't have to. Tom was as vulnerable as a puppy. All it took was a word here, a word there, to convince him that he was a nothing. I don't know why she felt she had to do that. Maybe she wasn't sure enough of her hold over Matthew, maybe she thought this time she'd really lose him. Whatever the reason, she did a thorough job. I tried to pick up the pieces. But it was no good. He was staying with me and I'd gone to the studio one day. He seemed calmer and I thought: Maybe he's over it. When I got back I found him in the garage. He was swinging from the cross-beams. He'd hanged himself.'

Brand motioned towards the whisky bottle but Murray Pick brushed it aside. 'Don't worry, I can talk about it. It helps.'

'But I didn't get the impression that Ella even knew you before this film.'

'She didn't. I'd never met her, and Matthew only briefly. They didn't know the connection. Tom used a stage name. Harper. He said it would look better in lights. I got the story from Tom and some other people who'd worked with him during the show. And after he was dead I was just numb. After all, nothing could bring him back. Until—I saw her on the balcony yesterday, humming that song. And I hated her. I hated her for all Tom's lost years.'

'You'd have killed her for a boy who committed suicide?'

'Not just any boy. Tom was my young brother. I'd practically brought him up. Didn't I say that?' He looked bemused. 'No, maybe not.'

'But why Ella? Why not Matthew? He was the one who ditched your brother, whether he wanted to or not.'

A sad smile crept over Murray Pick's stricken face. 'You can't blame Matt. That would be like arresting the Smith and Wesson instead of the killer who fired the shot. If only she hadn't started humming that tune! But in the event it didn't mean anything, did it? I wasn't the only one who hated her that much. Always supposing you believe what I've told you.'

Brand sighed. 'It doesn't much matter what I believe. But when you go to the police, I'll do what I can. You know you've no option now.'

'I know. And I imagine I'll be the prime suspect. Clever Ella! Even when she's dead she gets her revenge.' Then the self-pity suddenly gave way to a futile attempt at self-preservation. 'Look, Brand, if they think it's an accident . . . If there's no evidence . . .'

'Don't delude yourself. The police aren't fools. When they've reason to suspect foul play they'll find the evidence.'

'And you intend to give them the reason.'

Brand shook his head. 'No, you will. That is, if you have any sense you will. It'll be a whole lot easier for you if you volunteer your information.

His eyes followed Murray Pick as the man stood up, steadied himself on the back of the chair and then walked towards the window. He looked out at the night sky as if seeking an answer for his dilemma. 'I knew I never should have taken this movie. Salzburg. *The Sound of Music*. But I hadn't another picture lined up. That's the trouble with this business. You live from picture to picture and if there isn't one in the offing you get nervous. That's when you make mistakes. You think of the bloody money and . . .' He turned round abruptly. 'You're right, Brand. I'll turn myself in first thing.'

Brand sighed. 'Forget the drama. It's not *Starsky and Hutch*. You're simply giving the police relevant information. You're not being arrested or charged.' As he said it he became aware that the man was staring at him with a curious expression in his eyes.

'Why are you so involved in this? Why do you care?'

'I've been asking myself that all evening. Everything I've heard about Ella Armstrong should make me dislike her intensely. But I spent most of the day with her. She was a strange and difficult woman, but there was something about her. I suppose you could say I felt sorry for her.'

'Then you must be a minority of one.'

He thought about that when Murray Pick had left him. What a lonely way to die, so unloved! All she had to hang on to was Matthew Armstrong's need for her as the buffer between him and the less pleasant demands of his career. He was still thinking about her when he finally fell into a troubled sleep from which he awoke unrefreshed, barely noticing that it was a peerless morning of blue skies and warm sunshine. Checking his watch, he realized he'd slept far later than he'd intended.

Leo Kiesler looked concerned when Brand presented himself at his office in the Salzburg police station. 'You look a little under the weather, Ralph.'

'So would you if you'd had the night I had.'

'I've already gathered that. A man named—' he glanced at the pad on his desk—'Murray Pick, someone on the film unit, called in, told me quite an interesting story.'

'That's a relief.' Brand sat down heavily. 'I could do with a cup of your coffee. Black. What did you make of it? You're not holding him?'

'No, just cautioned him to make himself available when we needed him,' said Kiesler as he set the coffee down in front of Brand. 'We've seen Armstrong too. He looked about as lively as you do. Incidentally, Ralph, I'd appreciate it if you didn't go around representing yourself as a messenger for me.' He raised his hand, warding off Brand's apology. 'That's the least of my problems. It seems you were right. When you'd left last night I heard from the police surgeon after he'd completed his examination of the body.'

'And he found shreds of skin and possibly dried blood under her fingernails?'

'How did you know that?'

'A hunch.'

Kiesler nodded. 'Then you'd better give me some basis for your hunch. With this and Pick's evidence, we have to at least consider the possibility that she was deliberately pushed backwards and then held underwater to make sure she was dead.'

'*The Sound of Murder*. Reality writ in film clichés!'

'What was that?' Kiesler looked puzzled.

'Just something someone said.'

Kiesler shrugged. 'We've been interviewing those members of the film crew who were around at the time. Not much to go on there. It's not going to be easy. The producer insists on continuing filming and frankly we've no grounds for preventing him. Meanwhile, a bunch of newspaper reporters have flown in. You know what they'll be like if they get a sniff of a murder investigation. And on top of that Armstrong is worried stiff about something. Why the hell didn't he inform us he was changing hotels last night?'

'Didn't he tell you?'

'Tell me what?'

'He had a visitor from England. Young chap. Martin Elliott. Wasn't he with him when you saw him?'

'No. Just his agent. He'd been in Vienna with another client and caught the early train when he'd heard about the wife's death. You mean the marriage was just a front?'

'There was more to it than that. But he *is* homosexual. I gather it's well known in the business but it wouldn't do his image any good if it became public knowledge. That could be why he's worried. Unless . . .'

'Well, come on, Ralph, out with it.'

After Brand had finished speaking Kiesler instructed the sergeant in the outer office to call the Stadt Hotel.

While they waited he paced the room with measured strides, stopping at intervals as if he were about to utter, then thinking better of it. 'Where?' he said finally.

Brand caught his drift immediately. 'Grinzing!'

'Grinzing!' Kiesler repeated with an exasperated wave of the hand. 'That was fifty years ago, Ralph. I've sent a man down there to see what he can find out about her. But what's this obsession with Grinzing? Why not here and now? Armstrong, this man Elliott, the producer Schneider, maybe Murray Pick was fobbing us off with a plausible story about finding her dead and someone leaving the room. They all had motives.'

He was stopped in his tracks by a call from the sergeant. He listened intently, then slammed down the phone as if it had done him an injury. 'Martin Elliott left this morning. With his luggage. Film or no film, Armstrong's got some questions to answer,' he said grimly.

'I'd better leave you to get on with it, then.' Brand paused at the door. 'You'll let me know.'

Kiesler seemed confused for a moment. 'What? Oh— Grinzing! I'll let you know.' Already he'd consigned Ella Armstrong's distant past to the debris of history.

Then he called Brand back. 'Might be useful if you came out to the location with me. You saw this fellow Elliott last night and Armstrong might talk more freely to you than to me. I don't want to play the heavy detective —yet.'

'He's actually working today?' Remembering the state of the man the night before, let alone the fact that his wife had died violently less than twenty-four hours ago, Brand couldn't conceal his amazement.

'I know. It surprised me too. Apparently he insisted. Or maybe his agent or the producer insisted for him. Work is the best therapy for grief—that sort of thing.' He shook his head. 'No wonder they say there's no business like show business. Crazy people!'

During the trip to the villa location in the fast police car, driven by a young officer who supposedly fancied himself as a formula one champion, Kiesler remained deep in

thought and Brand kept his own counsel. Despite the buffetting of the car as it took the sharp curves of the road at
breakneck speed, he felt pleasantly drowsy and had to fight
off the urge to sleep by opening the window, hoping the
crisp mountain air would clear his brain.

Soon the villa in its picturesque setting surrounded by
the mobile clutter of the film unit came into view. There
were many more cars parked by the roadside than on the
day he'd visited previously.

As Kiesler's car was nodded through the gates by what
Brand took to be a plain clothes policeman, he noticed
Armstrong, flanked by Jake Schneider, Frederica Hubble
and a smooth, silver-haired man in a dark business suit he
hadn't seen before, in the centre of a group of reporters with
tape-recorders and notebooks. All around them photographers were snapping away from various contorted angles.

Not far off Lotte Bruckner was seated serenely on a folding
chair which might have been a throne for the majesty she
conferred on it. The make-up woman, who had been daub-
ing mock blood on Armstrong and Jeremy Fox when last
he'd seen her, was fussing over that formidable, timeless
face which needed no cosmetic embellishment. There was
a faraway look in the actress's eyes as she watched the
circus of Press and publicity surrounding her co-star. Brand
wondered what thoughts were going through her mind now
that Ella, the woman she'd turned on so harshly, was dead
and vowed he'd find out somehow.

But before he could do anything about it he was spotted
by Armstrong who whispered something to the silver-haired
man and then, composing his face into an expression of sad
fatigue, allowed himself to be disengaged from the mob.
Robbed of its quarry, the Press turned its attention less
enthusiastically to Jake Schneider.

As he strode towards the car Armstrong's face hardened.

'I want a word with you, Brand. What did you say to
Martin last night? He's gone!' Then he pulled back as he

took stock of the police car and realized the other occupant was Kiesler. 'Oh my God!' he cursed.

'That's what I wanted to talk to you about, Mr Armstrong,' said Kiesler agreeably.

Armstrong looked from the inspector to Brand. 'You bastard!' he muttered fiercely.

CHAPTER 12

'Cool it, Matt!'

The whispered warning caught Brand's ear before he saw the figure of the silver-haired man looming up behind Armstrong. He placed a protective arm around the actor's shoulders and directed a confidential smile first at Brand, then at Kiesler, nicely judged to convey both trust in their ability to understand the strain that had provoked Armstrong's reckless reaction and support for his client in his distress.

'I'm sure you can appreciate how Mr Armstrong is feeling just now.' His voice was as well groomed as his appearance, silky yet authoritative: he might have been fashioned by a casting editor for the role of a successful professional man with the hidden reserves of a trouble-shooter.

From the tone of his reply it appeared even Kiesler seemed to find him faintly intimidating. His words of sympathy sounded palpably sincere: the assurance that the questions he needed to ask were merely a formality came almost as an afterthought. As he spoke he looked meaningfully at Brand, who took the hint. He ducked his head to hide his admiration for Kiesler's smooth change of tactics to allay any fears Armstrong might be harbouring.

His words had the intended calming effect on Armstrong. Taking his cue from his companion, he apologized for his earlier display of temper, citing the strain of dealing with

the Press as an explanation. Certainly the pressure showed
on his face, although how much of that was due to a
monumental hangover Brand wasn't sure.

'I don't know what I'd have done without Allan. You
haven't met my agent, Brand. Allan Pennington.' There
was still a residue of suspicion in his eyes as he introduced
Brand.

'Perhaps we can talk somewhere privately,' said Kiesler,
nodding disparagingly at the cluster of media reporters
badgering Fred Hubble and Jake Schneider.

Armstrong looked imploringly at Pennington. 'I'd rather
Allan . . .'

'Oh, come now, Matt, I don't think the inspector wants
me present. As he says, it's just a formality.' Pennington
sounded affable but there was a steely undertone in his voice.
'Why don't you take Inspector Kiesler to your caravan? I'll
see you're not disturbed there.'

As the two men picked their way through the reporters,
photographers and the disgruntled film crew waiting for the
hubbub to subside so that they could continue shooting,
Pennington turned to Brand. 'Poor Matt! It's lucky I was
in Vienna and could get here quickly. I warned him what
it would be like. He really shouldn't have turned up today.
On the other hand, he was bound to be plagued by the Press
and perhaps it was better to get it over with straight away.
He did very well—considering.'

'Considering his wife is dead? Or that Martin Elliott left
this morning?'

Pennington raised an elegant eyebrow. 'Now what can
you possibly mean by that, Mr Brand? You don't think
Martin had anything to do with Ella's death?'

'No, I think someone cautioned him that it might be wise
in Matthew's best interests to make himself scarce. And
being an accommodating young man, he agreed.'

Brand studied Pennington's face for some kind of furtive
reaction. Instead a self-congratulatory smile played around

the man's mouth, giving him a faintly feline look. He inspected his immaculately tailored lapel and flicked off a minute speck of dust with a polished fingernail.

'You can't be too careful in this business,' he admitted with no hint of contriteness. 'That's what an agent's for—taking care of his client's interests. The Press can be very cruel, even when they think they're being kind.'

'Does Matthew know you sent Elliott packing?'

'For the moment, no. It hardly seemed necessary. I'm sorry he cast you as the villain.' He sounded amused. 'Later he'll see the sense of it. As I'm sure you do, Mr Brand,' he added deliberately. 'He's got enough on his plate without newspaper speculations about what he was doing shacking up with a young man on the evening his wife died.'

'You realize it puts Elliott in a difficult position. Naturally, the police will want to know why he disappeared so suddenly.'

Pennington waved a dismissive hand. 'Why should it bother them? After the funeral, it'll all die down.'

'I wouldn't be too sure of that, Mr Pennington.'

For the first time Brand felt he'd caught Pennington off guard. 'You're not suggesting there was anything suspicious about her death?'

Feeling no shame, Brand enjoyed the effect his words had on Pennington, puncturing that confident self-esteem. 'It's not for me to suggest anything. That's up to the Austrian police.'

'But if this got out! Matthew's career! Good God, it's taken long enough to get it off the ground. I oughtn't to have let that inspector loose on him alone.' He made no attempt to disguise his agitation.

'It's too late now, I'm afraid. Anyway he seems to have sobered up nicely. Last night be looked as if he'd swallowed the dog.'

Pennington stared back at him, blankly.

'That bit him,' Brand elaborated.

'Oh! Yes, well, he has a pretty fair capacity, like most actors. But never when he's working,' he said, preoccupied less with his client's drinking habits than with his chances of survival as a bankable show business commodity.

'How did you manage it? Phone call early this morning, while Matthew was still sleeping it off?'

Pennington nodded, absent-mindedly. 'Matt had let me know where he was staying yesterday. I say, Brand, I promise you it was done from the best motives. I mean, I couldn't be held in any way accountable.'

Brand shrugged. 'Not unless you had any reason for wanting Ella Armstrong dead—or, at least, out of the way.'

'What a crazy idea, man! Ella and I . . .' He stopped suddenly, seemingly realizing the futility of falsifying his relationship with the dead woman. 'We had our disagreements, of course. She seemed to think she could handle Matt's career better than I could. I! Who'd nursed him along through all the bad years. Then when he got his break, she . . . Well, you met her, she wasn't the easiest person to deal with. I told Matt, time and again, he shouldn't rely on her judgement so much.'

'Her judgement didn't seem to have done him much harm in the long run. If you want my advice, Mr Pennington, I think you should tell Inspector Kiesler everything you've told me.'

'Perhaps you're right. After all, I've my reputation to think of, too.' He straightened himself up. 'If I'd known what a jam Matt had got himself into, I'd have left him to it.' Suddenly his client's best interests seemed of less concern that his own.

Across the way he watched Armstrong and Kiesler emerge from the actor's caravan. 'Matt!' he called, leaving Brand unceremoniously as he hurried off in their direction, fending off Jake Schneider who had also witnessed the arrival of Kiesler with some anxiety.

The capable Fred Hubble was left to cope with final

demands from the reporters for 'just one more word with Matt,' 'one more picture' from the photographers. 'I'm sorry, everyone, that's it, Matthew won't be giving any more interviews. If there's anything else you need to know, you can ask me.' Efficiently, she marshalled them towards the facility tent for drinks, away from the director Barry Butler and the film crew who breathed a sigh of relief now that they could get back to the business of making the movie.

As Kiesler passed Brand with Allan Pennington in tow he lowered his right eyelid in the suspicion of a wink. Presumably his chat with Matthew Armstrong had proved fruitful.

'Mr Pennington and I are returning to town. Do you want a lift, Ralph?'

Brand scratched his chin as if considering the invitation. 'No, I think I'll hang around for a bit. I can probably cadge a lift later.'

He didn't mention that he was content to bide his time patiently, waiting for the opportunity to approach the enigmatic woman who'd been observing Armstrong's press conference so imperturbably. Lotte Bruckner.

It was well after the lunch-break, which Brand shared with a subdued Murray Pick and a generous pork chop and sauerkraut, that the last persistent members of the Press departed and shooting got underway.

'Bloody man, Schneider! It was his brilliant idea to stage that little charade for the reporters. I hope he's satisfied,' grumbled the make-up girl as the lighting cameraman and crew lined up for the next shot and Barry Butler took Lotte Bruckner and Armstrong through their paces.

'He will be,' said Fred Hubble in passing. 'Matt was terrific. You'd really think he minded that Ella was dead.'

Brand cocked his head at her. 'Doesn't he?'

'You mustn't pay too much attention to me, Mr Brand. I'm a natural born sceptic. It goes with the job,' she replied, leaving Brand to put whatever interpretation he liked on her remark.

As the day wore on Brand found himself increasingly impressed by the concentrated way in which the cast and crew managed to shrug off the morning's aggravation Schneider had wished on them, devoting themselves single-mindedly to putting on film the script-writers' fiction. It was as if, for them, the real world had ceased to exist.

Only Schneider seemed unnaturally edgy, causing the even-tempered director to explode. But it was all over in a few moments. A surprisingly meek Schneider retired, perching himself beside Brand on a low skirting wall behind the camera. He alternately nursed his paunch and dabbed his damp forehead with a handkerchief. Whatever was on his mind appeared to have nothing to do with the altercation or indeed the progress of the movie which was now woefully behind schedule.

'That inspector of yours, Brand, he wants to see me about something. Do you know what he wants? What's he doing poking around here? I had New York on the phone this morning. The heavy mob is coming over.'

'The heavy mob?'

'Executives from head office of the distribution company that's putting up most of the financing. That could be bad news. Christ, it's all bad news.' There was little trace of the self-assured man of the night before in his nervous ramblings. 'Still, Matt handled himself pretty well. We should get some decent coverage.'

'Quiet, everyone,' barked the first assistant director. 'It's a take.'

Grateful for the respite, Brand watched the scene unfolding from his vantage spot out of camera range. It was a tracking shot following Lotte Bruckner as she emerged from the villa, walked unhurriedly across the drive to confront Armstrong, who'd imagined himself unobserved and started when he saw her. 'Herr Braddock, you're trespassing.

You've no right to invade my privacy,' she said evenly. Despite the banal dialogue, her silvery voice intriguingly accented cast a spell over the unit. Her slightest gesture, the twitch of a shawl, a raised eyebrow, the turn of her head, the hand gripping an elaborately carved walking stick, wove instant magic. It was obvious as the scene continued that all eyes in the audience would be focused on her. Through take after take she managed to vary her performance minutely, refreshing it with some new movement or intonation. By comparison Armstrong seemed stodgy.

When she'd finished and Butler had pronounced himself satisfied, there was an uncanny quiet, then one after another the crew clapped.

Brand looked around amazed. He didn't think things like this occurred on movies. Those beefy prop men and electricians standing around caught up in the excitement of the fantasy they'd helped to produce and admiration for the woman who had given it life.

He turned to Schneider who, for a while, had shelved his own troubles and succumbed to the magic of Lotte Bruckner.

'Does this happen often?' asked Brand.

'Hardly ever. But just sometimes . . . you saw for yourself. Wait till New York sees the rushes!' he enthused, and rushed over to Barry Butler who was beaming with pleasure.

The scene seemed to galvanize actors, director and crew, as if, anxious to hang on to a lucky streak, they put their backs into getting maximum value out of the day that had started so badly.

By the time the light was fading, Barry Butler was hugging himself with pleasure and Brand overheard him exulting 'Five minutes in the can. Five gorgeous minutes in the can. Lotte, you were magnificent.' The woman inclined her head graciously. 'Good work, Matt,' he added as an afterthought. The latter smiled ruefully. He'd done his best but the opposition was unbeatable. Even so, he too seemed to be basking in the reflected glory. Brand marvelled at the way the actor had immersed himself so totally in his job when the cameras rolled, becoming a quite other person distanced from the traumatic concerns of Matthew Armstrong. Then quite suddenly he sagged as the reality he'd kept at bay flooded in. He looked desperately alone. No Ella. No Martin. Not even the dubious support of Allan Pennington. Although unsure whether he would be welcome, Brand felt compelled to offer some word of comfort. But before he could reach Armstrong, Fred Hubble, concern in her eyes, had moved across to the actor's side. Whatever her reservations about him, she responded to the crying need of another human being.

In the bustle of packing up for the night, Lotte Bruckner stood on the terrace, unapproachable, imperious, a gratified smile on her face. As she turned her shawl slipped from her shoulders. She bent awkwardly to pick it up but Brand was there before her. It was now, he thought, or never. 'Allow me, Frau Bruckner.' She looked at the shawl, then at Brand. 'Fraülein' she corrected him, taking the shawl from his hand.

She was still smiling, but there was a questioning look in her eyes. 'You are the policeman friend of Mr Armstrong, aren't you? I saw you the other day.' Unlike the modern breed of film-makers, she belonged to the old school, observing the formality of surnames even with colleagues.

She seemed to be waiting for some response from Brand, not merely an acknowledgement of his identity.

'I'd like to talk to you about Ella Armstrong,' he said abruptly, realizing that she could dismiss him instantly but gambling that she wouldn't.

She stared at him for a long, hard moment. Then she flicked the shawl over her shoulders with a practised flourish. 'My car is the dark blue Mercedes. Perhaps you'd like to wait for me,' she said, almost as if she'd been expecting him.

As she turned, Barry Butler bustled up to her, ignoring Brand. 'That was beautiful, Lotte,' he repeated effusively.

'We may have to dub the dialogue in the studio later, but everything else . . . what can I say?'

He was rewarded with that tantalizing smile, but her reply was crushing. 'You ask so little, Mr Butler. It was just a job of work.' The young director looked so crestfallen that Brand felt sorry for him. In a few words she had not only put him in his place but delivered a precise and damning assessment of his movie. Beneath that fastidiously elegant exterior there's one tough lady, thought Brand.

On the way back to the Mariahof where, it transpired, Schneider had secured for her the hotel's most luxurious suite, she purposely steered off the subject of Ella Armstrong, regaling him airily with reminiscences of the old days when she'd worked with the best directors in the best productions.

'I suppose one must move with the times, but these new film-makers, they talk about authenticity and all it means is transporting a unit to the actual location of the plot and spending vast amounts of money shooting the film on the spot. That's not authenticity. We used to build Vienna or Salzburg or Berlin in the studio and no one could tell the difference. It's here, this is where the authenticity should be.' She thumped her copy of the script of *The Sound of Murder*. 'It all stems from the words and if the words are no good . . . pooh!'

'Of course I'm a layman . . .' Brand began to say.

'You're the *public*. Did you care that Selznick burnt Atlanta on the back lot of the studio for *Gone With The Wind*, that my darling Max Ophuls created provincial Austria to the last minute detail on a sound stage in Hollywood for *Letter From An Unknown Woman?* It was the feeling, the emotion, the passion that mattered. The actors had size in those days. Matthew Armstrong—he's a professional, good for Television. But he has no size.' So much for Armstrong's dream of superstardom, thought Brand.

'Why did you decide to come out of retirement to make this film, then?' he ventured.

She shrugged her shoulders. 'I was bored. And—I needed the money. Schneider was very persuasive. He's a foolish, interfering man, acting as if he can do everyone's job better than they can. But he talks a good "deal", as they say in America. I shouldn't have come back to Salzburg,' she said suddenly. 'Memories, memories!'

'Ella Armstrong had memories, too,' Brand said quietly. 'She revered you, you know. Why did you treat her so cruelly?'

She turned to look at Brand. 'Were you spying on me?'

If Brand were capable of blushing he would have done so. 'Hardly spying,' he excused himself. 'I overheard. In your dressing-room. The little summerhouse.'

'Ah, that. You *were* spying. But why should I condemn you? When I was the guilty one.'

His silence seemed to irritate her, as if he were an actor who had forgotten his next line. 'Aren't you shocked?'

'You're the second person who has said that to me today. Everyone seemes to want to shock me. And for the second time: no, I'm not shocked, just curious.' He supposed that if high drama was your stock in trade it coloured everything in your life.

She nodded. 'When I heard she was dead I was grateful. But then I talked to the make-up woman about her. Film crews are great gossips. If you listen long enough you find out what you need to know.'

'And what did you find out?'

She clasped her hands tightly together and he noticed for the first time that the once expressive hands showed crippling signs of arthritis. 'That Ella Armstrong was the wrong woman,' she said.

CHAPTER 13

As she stepped out of the car and into the lobby of the Mariahof, her regal bearing skilfully disguising her gingerly movements, she motioned to Brand.

'I'd invite you up to my suite, but I invite no one to my suite except my maid. Privacy, at least, is the privilege of age.'

She gestured towards Fritz, the head porter, without actually acknowledging his existence. 'A quiet table in the lounge, I think. Away from the film people when they return. You'll see to that.' It didn't seem to occur to her that her requirements wouldn't be instantly attended to and Brand doubted whether that confident assumption had ever failed her.

He followed her slow, courtly progress across the lounge to the discreet table indicated by Fritz, sheltered by a leafy display of potted palms from prying eyes.

Unlike other women, Lotte Bruckner didn't just sit down. She settled herself becomingly on the gilt settee, first checking the impression she was making in a convenient adjacent mirror before addressing her companion.

'Now, Mr . . .?'

'Brand.'

'It sounds German.'

'Without a "t".'

'Now, Mr Brand without a "t", how can I help you and why should I?' she said directly. Her tone implied that her time and her patience were limited and he'd better make good use of both.

'Why was Ella Armstrong the wrong woman?' he replied, matching her own straightforward approach.

She pursed her lips. 'I'd have thought that was obvious. I mistook her for someone else.'

'Someone who warranted your – wrath, for want of a better word?'

'Oh, much more than wrath, Mr Brand. That's too trivial a word.' As she studied him closely her attitude changed. The façade and contrivances of the public image dropped away, exposing a sad, haunted old lady.

There was no theatricality in her long silence. She seemed genuinely to be wrestling with a memory that was almost too painful to contemplate.

When she finally spoke, the words tumbled out as if she could no longer contain them. 'When Ella Armstrong came to see me – that day on the set – I was surprised but not annoyed. She told me how much she'd admired my work in the past. One's vanity is always open to flattery in this business. Then she told me she too had been born in the province in a village near here, Grinzing. She seemed to think that might be a bond between us. Then she said her maiden name was Ella Knödel, she made a joke of it.'

'And that name meant something to you?'

Although her eyes were focused on Brand he might have been any inanimate object. She wasn't seeing him. She was seeing the past that name had revived for her. 'Before the war, long before I became an actress, I was engaged to a young man, Ernst Hesselmann. His family were wealthy jewellers in Salzburg. They'd been established here for over a century. They owned a beautiful estate on the outskirts of Salzburg. My father was a local merchant and when he died my mother was quite poor. The Hesselmanns, the mother and father, Jacob and Hannah, who had known my father, were very good to us. They were charitable people. Ernst and I fell in love. Ernst's sister Leah was my best friend. The family was unusual in that they gave the engagement their blessing.'

'Why unusual? Because you were poor?'

'Because they were Jews and I was Christian. Jews usually marry Jews. But apart from the observances of their religion, I don't think they considered themselves of a different race. They were Austrian and proud of it. They saw what was happening in Germany when the Nazis came to power, but, like so many Jews, they couldn't believe it would happen to them. They were well respected in the community. I believed, as they did, that no harm would come to them in this civilized country.'

Even now over a distance of fifty years, her mouth trembled and there was a suggestion of tears in those magnificent eyes. 'When there was talk of an *Anschluss*, I remember Herr Hesselmann saying that the excesses of the Nazis, their treatment of the Jews, wouldn't happen on the same scale in Austria. Austrians always tend to regard Germans as vulgarians, you see. In any case, he said, it would all die down. Every new government has a scapegoat, but once it's established we have to live together in peace. Poor man, now I wonder how he could have been so blind.'

'And what happened to the Hesselmanns?' Brand prompted, although he knew what had to be the answer.

She drew a deep breath. 'Too late they realized that the pattern in Germany was being repeated in Austria, if anything it was worse. After the *Anschluss*, the new authorities started victimizing the Jews, especially those with influence and money, flourishing businesses. And, most especially, those like Jacob Hesselmann who didn't hide his distaste for the Nazi regime. People they thought were their friends suddenly weren't available any more. It was obvious that to survive they had to leave. Jacob made some sort of deal with the local Nazi ministry to allow the family safe passage abroad. They had friends in America and when they were settled I was to join them and Ernst. They were allowed to take no goods, no money, with them. The business would be turned over to the Nazis. But Jacob was naive enough to think he could smuggle some uncut diamonds of great value out with them, sufficient to start up a new business abroad. The diamonds weren't listed in the inventory, so there was no record of their existence. He devised ways of transporting them. In the hollow heels of his wife's shoes. Only I, who was practically a member of the family, knew of the plan outside the Hesselmanns. At least, that's what we thought.'

'But someone else knew?'

'Or made it her business to find out. Hannah's maid. Elke Knödel. You don't forget a surname like that. But over the years I'd confused her given name with Ella.'

'Elke was her sister?'

'I realized my mistake after Ella's death when I learned that she'd never been in service and at the time I'm speaking of she'd married and was in America.'

'Did this Elke have a grudge against the Hesselmanns?'

'Who knows? I doubt it. You must remember the atmosphere then, or imagine it. The Nazis got to the young first. It was their duty to inform against anyone – employers, even parents – for the good of the state. And the Jews especially were the enemy. There was no such thing as a good Jew. If they'd treated you well it was just to soften you up, to corrupt the true Aryan spirit that would be the salvation of Germany and Austria. The girl had obviously learned the lesson well. She informed the authorities that Jacob was planning to smuggle jewels out of the country. They didn't need any other evidence. On the day before the family was about to leave, they were all arrested – Jacob, Hannah, Ernst, Leah. For a long time I heard nothing, then I learned they'd been sent to Dachau concentration camp in Germany. That was the last. Years after the war, I got word that they'd been transported eventually to one of the death camps. They were all dead. Everyone who'd worked for them, loyal employees, were interrogated. So was I. But I was a Christian, an Aryan and, to my shame, a coward. Some of the workmen on the estate stood up for the Hesselmanns and paid for it. I – I said nothing. I simply answered their questions and they seemed satisfied. Soon after that I left for Vienna and embarked on my career as an actress. I was frightened, you see, like so many people. But fear, Mr Brand, fear is no excuse,' she said bitterly.

Watching the proud woman struggling to control the emotions generated by that grim reminder of a haunted past was more disturbing to Brand than if she'd broken down and wept. He offered his hand in a tentative gesture of comfort but she brushed it aside. Having borne this burden in silence all these years, she was too old, too self-contained, to invite sympathy now.

'Why do you reproach yourself? What could you have done?' he asked lamely, knowing she must have asked herself those questions many times and received no blameless answers.

'It was a sin of omission, Mr Brand. I should have stood up and been counted. It wouldn't have saved the Hesselmanns but it might have saved me. The part of me that matters. The soul. When you start collaborating with – or simply ignoring – evil, it becomes easier and easier. During the war years when I became a successful actress in Vienna and then Berlin, I could convince myself I wasn't a Nazi. What had I to do with their atrocities? I was merely doing my job. How could I change anything by refusing to use the talent and gifts I'd been given? But deep down I felt as guilty as that silly, dangerous girl, Elke Knödel.'

'That's absurd,' said Brand softly.

'I know it's absurd. My mind says it's absurd. But my heart knows it isn't. I never married and I still mourn for Ernst. Only when I act, when I become another person, can I forget – just for a little while. I've never spoken like this to anyone before and I don't think I intended to now. Perhaps it's all that has happened here in the past few days. Perhaps I just wanted someone to ask me why? Or who is Lotte Bruckner really? And you happened to be that someone. Although I suspect you're rather good at persuading people to reveal themselves.'

Brand inclined his head, not sure whether he was being complimented or reprimanded.

'Did you hate Elke Knödel enough to have wanted to kill her?'

She looked at him steadily. 'I hated her once. Now I pity her. And I wouldn't have wanted to kill her. If she's alive she's had to live with her conscience all this time. That's punishment enough. I know.'

'Are there any other people who worked for the Hesselmanns, who felt as strongly as you did, still living?'

She thought for a moment, surprised at his question. 'I know of only one. Otto Viertel. He was Leah, the daughter's, music tutor. An old friend. He was one of the brave ones. He was a brilliant musician. But the Nazis destroyed him. He survived the concentration camps, but he was a physical wreck. They patched him up after the war and because he had relatives in America he was able to get a visa to go abroad. But the outside world was too much for him. He returned to Salzburg. We all come home to roost – or to die. He ekes out a kind of living teaching music.'

'Have you seen him lately?'

'No, but I'd intended visiting him while I was here. Why . . .?' Then the puzzled frown that creased her forehead cleared. 'You believe Ella Armstrong was murdered. Because of her sister!'

Brand nodded. 'It's very likely. Isn't it possible that someone else made the same mistake as you did?'

'I can't believe that.' She sounded confused.

Brand pressed his point. 'You don't mean that, do you? Fräulein Bruckner, would you shield a killer, even if you understood why they had committed murder?'

She took a deep breath, holding her head erect as he'd seen her do on the screen when she was making an unpalatable but righteous admission. 'No. There's been enough death. If I learned anything from the Hesselmanns in their goodness it was the charity of forgiveness. At least, I try. Even though – poor Ella! – I don't always succeed.'

'Have you any idea what happened to Elke Knödel after she turned in the Hesselmanns?'

She smiled that small bitter smile. 'No. But I'm sure she was well rewarded. The Nazis were very generous to their informants.'

They were interrupted by an apologetic cough. Locked in a past that seemed more vivid than the present, they suddenly realized that the head porter had been trying discreetly to attract Brand's attention.

He bowed his head respectfully to Lotte Bruckner before addressing himself to Brand. 'Inspector Kiesler called, sir. He asked you to telephone him as soon as possible.'

'Thank you, Fritz. Did he say anything else?'

'No, sir. I told him you were busy. I hope that was correct. And he simply asked that you make contact with him.'

Brand nodded, watching the upright figure disappearing across the lounge in his loden green jacket to sort out some routine altercation between a guest and a page boy who had delivered the wrong luggage to his room.

When he turned back to Lotte Bruckner she was regarding him with interest and there was a curious alertness in her eyes.

'Do you call all Austrian porters Fritz, like Americans call all cab drivers "Bud"?'

He wasn't sure whether she was mocking him, as if the man she'd so recently confided in had turned into a figure of fun and, despite himself, he felt aggrieved.

'No,' he replied curtly. 'I call him that because it's his name. Fritz Sommer. I asked him.'

She studied the misshapen joints of her infirm hands pensively. 'Strange!'

He had no way of knowing to what she was referring and her next remark abruptly terminated the conversation. 'You must telephone your Inspector Kiesler and I have things to do, Mr Brand.'

Something in her tone worried Brand and he had the feeling that she was holding back, withdrawing from him. Perhaps, like Ella, she now regretted having revealed so much of her life to him. But he doubted whether she'd appreciate the irony that in many ways they were much alike and not only in their age and birthplace.

He made an attempt to reach her again while realizing that it would be useless. 'If there's anything else you know or suspect about Mrs Armstrong's death . . .'

'I know nothing.' She cut him short. 'I must go now.'

'Where?' he said, hoping the bluntness of his query would prompt a frank answer.

'It's none of your business,' she replied coldly. 'But since you ask, I shall visit my friend Otto Viertel.'

Brand felt that prickle of unaccountable fear shoot up his spine which he learned in the past not to ignore. 'Don't . . .' he began.

'I don't need advice from you, Mr Brand.' Then she seemed to relent. 'I must see Otto.'

'Take care, Fräulein Bruckner,' he said quietly. 'May I accompany you?'

'No, you may not, Mr Brand. I'm perfectly capable of taking the short walk to Otto's apartment in my own city. The air will do me good, clear my mind. I'm not a cripple – yet.'

She rose to her feet with a care for her ageing muscles that she seemed to transform into a kind of gracefulness. She held out her hand and beneath the cool, dry skin he realized it was shaking very slightly. 'I have enjoyed our conversation,' she said, the trivial remark as final as a full stop. How like Ella, he thought. Twice dismissed by redoubtable Austrian ladies of advanced years.

And, again, he felt that *frisson* of alarm as he twinned the two women in his mind.

On the telephone Leo Kiesler was uncommunicative, but his lack of an explanation for wanting to see Brand urgently was in itself explanation enough.

As he neared the now familiar headquarters of the Salzburg police, Brand was struck once more by the incongruity of the charming setting juxtaposed with the mission in which he was involved. The city of music, with its little girls in dirndls, stately matrons in stout felt hats taking their evening constitutional, and carefree tourists in shorts and jogging suits, merged into a more ominous picture of vengeance and memory. Of storm troopers and Nazi emblems and bewildered Jews hounded out of a life they had thought to be inviolable.

For a moment he wanted to turn away. If retribution for that past, even if it were mistaken, was the cause of Ella's death he could feel only sympathy for the murderer. It was a sort of justice. But, even as he thought that, he knew he couldn't ignore the other justice for which he'd been trained, which had occupied the better part of his life. Right and wrong were moral issues for judges and juries. Mitigating circumstances. Murder was a crime and criminals must be apprehended. That was the policeman's creed – Kiesler's and Brand's.

As he stepped out of his taxi, he almost collided with Matthew Armstrong who was rushing blindly out of the police station, closely followed by Allan Pennington and another man who was trying vainly to restrain the actor.

'Armstrong!'

Matthew pulled himself up, recognizing Brand. His face was ashen, his eyes staring. 'Brand. Thank God! You've got to help me. They think I murdered Ella!'

CHAPTER 14

'Grab a hold of yourself, Matt!' Allan Pennington gripped Armstrong's shoulder, although he looked as shaken as his client. 'It's not that bad. Is it, Herr Heit?'

'Heiss!' The neat, precise man peering through owlish spectacles corrected him painstakingly in English spoken with a clipped, formal accent. 'Bruno Heiss!'

'Heiss. It's not, is it? That bad?'

'Of course not, Mr Pennington. The police are just "fishing", as you say.' He sounded clinically objective, as if the question were merely academic.

Armstrong looked at him helplessly. 'Well, they've damn well got me on the hook. Brand, for Christ's sake, you've got to do something. You know I wouldn't have harmed Ella.'

'Mr Armstrong, I don't think it advisable for you to discuss this matter with a third party.'

The advice was logical enough but in his state of mind Armstrong was in no condition to differentiate between a warning and a threat.

'What the bloody hell do you know about it?' He made a feeble lunge in the direction of the man, who retreated hastily. Between them, Pennington and Brand managed to restrain the actor. It required little effort. There was no real fight in Armstrong, only anger and disbelief.

'I'll do what I can,' Brand assured him.

'Mr Pennington, I really must ask you to control your client, it's doing his case no good,' said Bruno Heiss, adjusting his spectacles primly.

'He's right, Matt. Come on,' said Pennington, clearly embarrassed by the scene Armstrong had provoked and the interest it had aroused in a group of passing tourists.

'Isn't that Braddock, the man who plays Braddock?' said one of them in a penetrating English voice, as the two men hurried Armstrong into a waiting car.

'It was Braddock? Wasn't it?' Brand realized that the question was being addressed to him. 'Great TV series! Are they filming here? That was a rehearsal wasn't it?'

Brand faced the eager English tourists and nodded. 'Yes, that was Braddock. A sort of rehearsal.' He didn't add: a rehearsal for real.

He turned to the young officer who had escorted the three men out of the police station. 'What was that all about?' he ruminated to himself.

'*Bitte?*' the officer inquired politely.

'Never mind.'

Leo Kiesler was more forthcoming.

'I ran into Matthew Armstrong outside. He seems to think you're going to arrest him for murder,' said Brand.

Kiesler sighed. 'That's what comes of acting in a detective series on Television. Would I be letting him leave the station if he were being arrested?'

'All the same, you must have given him cause to think that. Who was that little chap with Pennington and him?'

'Bruno Heiss? I suggested to Pennington earlier today that Armstrong might need some legal advice. He'd agreed to come to the station after the day's filming and we have to be careful questioning visitors. Particularly distinguished visitors. Heiss has been acting for the film company in legal matters over here. He seemed the sensible, or at any rate the most available, choice for the moment. No doubt Armstrong will want to consult his own legal counsel from England in due course—should it be necessary.'

'Does he need legal advice?'

'It's possible. As in your police force, I have to convince my superiors that I've sufficient evidence to bring a charge and make it cling.'

'Stick.'

'Cling, stick—Ralph, it's been a hard day, don't you make it harder.'

He sounded weary, not like the usual spruce, alert Kiesler. Brand sympathized with his friend. From experience he knew that treading the delicate tightrope between doing your job while at the same time not offending influential people who could cause you unnecessary trouble was a trying exercise, requiring a tricky balance of patience and firmness.

'What have you got on him?' Brand persisted, but less forcefully now.

'When I interviewed him again I put it to him that he'd lied to you and to me about not seeing his wife that afternoon when she came back from your excursion. And he just caved in. It's amazing how the official atmosphere of a police station can loosen the tongue. No pressure, no third degree.' He smiled wryly. 'He admitted when she came back to her room she'd found him there packing a bag. She'd seen his friend, lover, whatever, Martin Elliott, in the hotel lobby and she was furious. They had a bitter argument. He said he lost control and raised his arm to strike her. She struck back at him, clawed his arm with her hand. That accounts for the plaster you saw on his wrist and the shred of skin and dried blood under her fingernails. Then, according to him, they both realized they were behaving childishly. It wasn't as if she didn't already know about Elliott. It was just the shock of seeing him in Salzburg, knowing Armstrong had invited him behind her back. You can believe that if you like. He lied before, he could be lying about that, too.'

'That's all?'

'That. And the location manager's evidence that he heard someone leave the room just before he found her dead in the bathtub. And he had a motive. Maybe he was fed up with living a lie. Maybe she wouldn't give him a divorce. Maybe she threatened to publicly expose his double life if he left her. I understand your British newspapers pay handsomely for memoirs like that.'

'And now what do you hope to achieve?'

'Give him a few hours to brood on it and I think he'll crack. Admit he waited until she was taking a bath and then pushed her under, cracking her skull on the taps. Not a neat or particularly foolproof method of murder. But you know as well as I that people aren't rational at times like that. In the event he was lucky. It worked. She died. And, if you hadn't been so persistent, Ralph, he might just have got away with it.'

'Lucky! That's an odd word. Luck is the last thing Armstrong has right now.' Brand slumped in his chair. He'd listened to Kiesler's precise summing up of the evidence with mounting disquiet. He imagined Armstrong probably feeling more alone than he'd ever felt before. He had no doubt that Allan Pennington would be only too anxious to wash his hands of him. Bruno Heiss would be no comfort. Jake Schneider would be more concerned about his movie, the film crew about their jobs if the production were abandoned.

'I wish I'd been a thousand miles from here when she died. I wish I'd never told you about Martin Elliott or the damned plaster on Armstrong's wrist,' he said angrily.

Puzzled, Kiesler walked round his desk and perched on the corner of it facing Brand. 'What are you saying, Ralph? This isn't like you.'

'Well, it is now. I'm convinced Armstrong no more killed his wife than I did. Of course he lied. People lie all the time for all kinds of reasons. If he breaks down and admits what you want him to admit it's because he's convinced himself it's true. Not because it *is* true.' He looked urgently at Kiesler. 'Ella Armstrong was murdered by mistake for something she *didn't* do nearly fifty years ago.'

As he told Kiesler of his conversation with Lotte Bruckner he sensed his friend's quickening interest, although his response was dubious. 'It's a familiar story. But it's all theory, Ralph.'

'But you agree I could be right?'

Kiesler scratched the stubble that had sprouted on his chin through the long, arduous day. When he spoke it was with a mixture of reluctance and sadness, like a man confessing to an old sin which persisted in surfacing however much he tried to bury it.

'You're not telling me anything I don't know, Ralph. Oh, not the Hesselmanns. An old man was found floating in the river, drowned, not many years ago. Nothing much was known about him until it was learned that he'd been a member of the SS active in rounding up enemies of the Reich for slave labour during the war. Verdict: accidental death. A woman was mugged and knifed to death in a quiet street. Nothing much was known about *her* prior to 1946, until someone discovered in the files that she'd been a *Kapo* —a prisoner guard—in Buchenwald. Case unsolved.'

He paused, monitoring Brand's reaction, which suggested he was two jumps ahead of Kiesler's story.

'The drowning may have been a genuine accident, the mugging and knifing a genuine chance tragedy,' the inspector went on. 'Or perhaps the hated SS man was run to earth and killed by a relative of one of his victims. Perhaps the brutal *Kapo* was waylaid and exterminated—for want of a better word—by a survivor from the concentration camp. Memories run deep. Until the Nazi misery is beyond human memory there'll always be a doubt. But without evidence . . . !' He shrugged his shoulders.

'And if there had been evidence you wouldn't have wanted to bring those people to justice anyway, would you?' Brand prompted him.

But Kiesler wasn't about to fall into that trap. 'I'm a policeman, Ralph. Just like you were. I'm not concerned with the "why?" of a crime.' Then he clapped his hands together in a gesture of irritation either at Brand's side-tracking tactics or his own willingness to be side-tracked. 'And all this is hypothetical. In this case it's far more logical that Armstrong is our man.'

Kiesler's confident assumption of Armstrong's guilt on fairly flimsy evidence struck Brand as curious, out of character with his friend's normally cautious methods, as if he were taking the line of least resistance.

'Leo,' he said quietly, 'admit at least there are alternatives. Lotte Bruckner knows something. I swear she does. She wouldn't tell me what, at least not until she'd spoken to this man Otto Viertel who'd worked for the Hesselmanns. You have to take seriously what I've been telling you. It's surely worth talking to her.'

Kiesler moved round his desk, opened a drawer and took out an envelope from which he extracted a faded photograph. He handed it to Brand. 'Does this answer any of your questions?'

Brand looked up at Kiesler thoughtfully. 'You weren't going to show me this, were you?' he challenged him.

'I hadn't made up my mind. After Armstrong, it didn't seem important.'

The camera imprint on the fragile paper showed a group of very young girls seated primly, hands in their laps, with a smiling nun in the centre. It was obviously a formal school photograph, the kind that used to be taken each term and then stuck in an album to be treasured or laughed at or forgotten over the years. Brand's eyes flicked over the faces of the children from right to left until they focused on one particular face, its bright eyes staring at the camera with that glassy look of suspended animation as the lens fixed the moment. More than fifty years later those taunting eyes hadn't changed.

Brand placed his forefinger on the face.

'It's Ella Armstrong.'

Kiesler smiled, shaking his head. 'No, it isn't. Look again.'

Surprised, Brand searched the other faces more closely.

At the far end of the group he found another face with the same brazen eyes, the same flaxen pigtails, the same assured expression.

'It's unbelievable!' His eyes swivelled from one girl to the other. .

'I know,' said Kiesler. 'That one is Ella.' He pointed to the girl on the end. 'This one—' he indicated the other face —'is her sister, Elke. They weren't twins, but apparently they looked as alike as two peas in a pod. Only in appearance, though. Their characters were quite different.'

'Where did you get this?'

'The officer I sent to Grinzing did a thorough job. He asked around and managed to locate one of the nuns who'd taught the girls. She's very old and infirm, cared for by the other nuns, but her mind is alert. The Reverend Mother allowed Kruger to see her. She remembered both girls. As with most teaching nuns, her pupils had been her life. She recalled that Ella had been wayward, a trial to her parents, and had been apprenticed as a seamstress in Salzburg. Elke had been meek and submissive and when she was old enough she'd left school to work for the Hesselmanns.'

'That's all?'

'That's all.'

'But this surely bears out my theory that if Lotte Bruckner had mistaken Ella for her sister, so could someone else.'

Kiesler took the photograph from his hand and returned it carefully to the envelope. 'We promised faithfully to return it to the nun. Sister Catherine. All it proves, Ralph, is that the two girls were uncannily alike when they were—what? —eleven, twelve years old. Ralph?'

Brand roused himself from a brown study haunted by two identical pairs of eyes frozen in a photograph over fifty years old. He got up from his chair so abruptly that it tipped over on to the floor.

'Ralph?'

'I'm sorry, Leo,' said Brand urgently as he righted the

chair. 'I'm wasting time. And so are you, only you won't admit it. I have to speak to Lotte Bruckner again.'

'What . . . ?'

'I don't know. If I did I wouldn't be so concerned.'

'You'll be needed for the inquiry—inquest,' Kiesler called as Brand made for the door.

'I'll be there,' Brand replied. Then he paused. 'And the funeral?'

'Pennington's making arrangements. She's to be buried in Salzburg.'

'That seems appropriate.' The irony in Brand's voice wasn't lost on the inspector.

On his way back to the Mariahof Brand tried to rationalize his sudden feeling of alarm. But however he argued it, he couldn't still the small warning voice inside him.

For the moment the hotel seemed unnaturally quiet, the lobby all but deserted. Fritz had been called away by the manager and the hall porter on duty was feeling hard done by at having to extend his shift. He spoke little English and seemed to take some pleasure in misunderstanding Brand. But eventually Brand got through to him that he wished to speak to Fräulein Bruckner.

Seconds ticked away as her telephone refused to answer.

'Try again,' said Brand.

The porter sighed, tried again, waited, fixing Brand with his bored, accusing eyes.

He realized he'd been too late to prevent her making her excursion to visit Otto Viertel and he braced himself for the laborious job of enlisting the porter's help in finding Viertel's address. Then after a useless exchange he cursed himself for not doing the obvious: looking it up in the telephone directory. I must be getting addled, he thought, as he thumbed through the book.

Otto Viertel was listed as a piano teacher residing in one of those small, placid back streets that seemed to have declared unilateral independence from the rest of modern

Salzburg. He'd remembered seeing it quite by chance on his walking tour of the city in that long-ago time three days before when he'd thought he'd come to Salzburg for a holiday. Lotte Bruckner had been right. It was within easy walking distance of the hotel.

As he thanked the porter curtly for his non-assistance, Brand prayed that he wasn't too late. For what? If he'd known that he'd have begged Kiesler to send a police car. He pushed his way brusquely through the idling groups of tourists, then out of the main square and through the side streets funnelling off the Franz-Josef-Strasse. Approaching the address he'd found in the telephone directory, he became aware of a commotion of some sort, surprising because the area had previously seemed so quiet, almost secretive, when he'd first spotted it. As he hurried closer, the commotion took on a shape: the distant buzz became voices raised in horror, mingling with the whine of an ambulance that inched its way through the huddle of people, whose eyes were focused on a lifeless body sprawled on the cobbled paving.

Brand elbowed his way to the centre of the group of bystanders, his eyes confirming what he already feared. The body was Lotte Bruckner's, lying in a pool of blood that stained the cobblestones a ghastly scarlet. Her legs were crumpled beneath her and one crippled hand still clasped the elegant cane. She looked strangely at peace, as if a long-borne burden had been lifted from her. 'She seems familiar. Famous, do you think?' An American boy, probably a student, was peering over Brand's shoulder.

Brand nodded. 'Yes, you could say she was famous.'

CHAPTER 15

The apartment house where Otto Viertel lived wore its patina of age with the faded dignity of a dowager who knew her best days were over but was too proud to admit it. It stood erect in the narrow street mocking its more modern and functional neighbours, the flaking stucco flourishes tarnished a smoky grey by time and weather. A plump, pink-faced woman peered at Brand suspiciously from a ground-floor window as he had difficulty deciphering the names of the tenants slotted into a column beside the front door. Some had been crossed through and others scrawled over them several times. None of them had been printed with particular care, as if the owners of the names were either reluctant to reveal themselves or didn't feel the need to do so.

The woman continued to stare at Brand as he finally decided that a fairly firm 'V' which petered out into an illegible scribble was more than likely meant to be Viertel who resided on the top floor. Then she rapped on the windowpane and motioned him angrily away, and as she did so he noticed a tabby cat seemingly glued to her shoulder glowering at him with equal intensity. Unsure whether to smile, explain or just ignore her, Brand was relieved when the front door opened and a boy and girl arm in arm spilled through it, laughing at some secret joke.

At the sight of them the woman and the cat in the window looked even more outraged. The young couple continued laughing, almost bumping into Brand. *'Hexe!'* the girl giggled.

'I'm sorry?'

She frowned, searching for an English word. 'Crazy?' She jiggled a forefinger by her right temple. 'You know?'

The scowling cat and woman retreated behind the lace curtains. The couple jostled each other down the street and Brand braced himself for the climb up the winding stone stairs to the top floor.

When he reached the final landing he paused, catching his breath after the long haul, conscious that his heart was pumping away furiously inside him. The combination of the strenuous climb, the strange woman and the laughing

youngsters had been as unnerving as the sight of Lotte
Bruckner's dead body in the street. He felt an odd sense of
dislocation, as if he'd wandered by chance into one of those
weird *avant garde* movies with no beginning or middle or
end, just a pervasive atmosphere in which past, present and
future were all muddled together.

He leaned heavily against the stout door of Otto Viertel's
apartment and rang the bell, almost wishing that it wouldn't
be answered and unsure what he'd say if it were. Hello, Mr
Viertel, your friend, Lotte Bruckner, is dead. Hello, Mr
Viertel, did you by any chance drive the car that killed
Lotte Bruckner? Hello . . .

'*Ja?*'

The door had opened a crack, revealing a pinched severe
face which might have been male or female.

'Herr Viertel?'

The door opened wider and Brand saw that the voice
belonged to a woman of indeterminate years with a tiny
but purposeful figure dressed in old-fashioned dark grey
bombazine. '*Ja!*' it admitted reluctantly. She looked as he
imagined Mrs Danvers in *Rebecca*, only less malign.

'Lisa?' Another voice called from the interior of the apartment, followed by a shuffling sound as someone traversed
the long, high-ceilinged corridor inside. Brand heard the
stick and the limping footsteps before he saw their owner.
The woman stood aside as the man made his slow, painful
progress to the door. He was a foot shorter than Brand and
all his strength seemed to have been sucked into willing his
crippled body to obey the commands of his brain. As he
looked up at the unexpected visitor, Brand found himself
gazing into a face that appeared to be divided into two
halves unrelated to each other.

One side was whole, unblemished except by the lines of
age, the other had caved in like a gaunt crater with a deep
scar streaking from his forehead to his misshapen chin. It
was the face of a cruelly disfigured gargoyle but for the

apparent serenity and gentleness of the eyes, which gave it humanity.

But the eyes didn't seek Brand's, they stared fixedly at a point beyond him. Only then did Brand realize that the man he wished to see was blind.

'Herr Viertel,' said Brand tentatively. '*Ich bin ein Freund —von Lotte Bruckner.*' The name elicited a spark of interest. '*Lotte! Hier. In Salzburg?*'

'*Sprechen sie Englisch?*' Brand doubted whether they'd get very far if Otto Viertel didn't.

'*Ja, ja!* Of course. Come in, please. Lisa, *Kaffee, bitte.*'

The woman looked doubtful but grudgingly motioned Brand along the corridor to a large, cluttered room at the end, first assuring herself that Otto Viertel was locating the landmarks of familiarity in his apartment with the sensitive hand on his good side.

Despite his infirmity he paced himself surely, edging into the large room and moving with slow certainty towards the leather-covered easy chair under the fanlight.

When she'd seen him comfortably settled she went into the kitchen, grumbling quietly to herself in German.

'Please, Mr . . . ?'

'Brand. Ralph Brand. I'm sorry, I should have introduced myself.'

'Mr Brand, sit down. The settee by the piano is quite restful. I know those stairs. There may be some music scores on it. Perhaps you could put them on the piano. My last pupil is very messy. But you can't expect the young and sighted to appreciate how important it is that I should know exactly where everything is. You mustn't mind Lisa. She's my cousin and housekeeper and far too protective of me. She thinks I should be in bed. Now, you have news of Lotte? She wrote she would be making a film in Salzburg, but I didn't know she was already here.'

'She didn't come to see you this evening?'

'No.' There was a rising tension in Otto Viertel's voice

as if he'd been anticipating the question. His answer disheartened Brand. If Lotte Bruckner had been killed before she'd managed to see her old friend, then Brand could only guess at her urgent reason for getting in touch with him.

His silence seemed more disturbing to Otto Viertel than a blind man's natural reaction to a sudden stillness he couldn't explain. He clutched the arm of his chair with his strong hand, waiting for Brand to speak. His unseeing eyes appeared to be trying to focus on his visitor, sensing perhaps that the news for which he'd asked must be bad.

'What is it you're not telling me, Mr Brand?'

'*Kaffee!*' The grim-faced little woman bustled in with a tray which she put in front of Brand after pouring a cup for Otto Viertel and carefully placing it within reach on the table beside his chair. He waved her aside irritably and, without acknowledging Brand's smile of thanks, she sniffed loudly and departed back to her kitchen.

'Mr Brand!'

'Lotte Bruckner is dead.' It came out more brutally than Brand had intended but he sensed that the man in front of him would prefer a direct truth directly stated. His thin body shrank even deeper into the well-worn velvet jacket which was several sizes too large for him. His sightless eyes glazed over. But there was no grief in his expression, only resignation. He had used up his capacity for suffering years ago, Brand judged.

'Poor Lotte!' he said finally. 'But then, none of us are getting any younger. I hadn't heard the radio. Was it a heart attack? An illness? She wrote frequently, though we didn't often see each other. She never mentioned . . .'

'I doubt whether it would have been on the radio yet,' Brand broke in. 'She was killed, seemingly by a hit-and-run driver. I imagine on her way to see you.'

Otto Viertel shook his head wearily. 'What a useless way to die!'

That's what the ambulance man had said, Brand remembered, as he'd covered that luminous face and lifted her body on to a stretcher. It had seemed an inadequate thing to say. Tragic! Appalling! Useless went without saying. Except, if what he'd feared were true, her death might be very useful to someone, perhaps the driver of the car or van that had apparently run her down as she stepped off the pavement in that quiet street. There'd been no witnesses and the ambulance man had muttered something about the dangerous corner, improperly signposted and too sudden access to the fast highway. 'Probably on his way to Munich or Innsbruck now,' he'd said. The American boy had translated for Brand and said he remembered now where he'd seen Lotte Bruckner. In an old movie at the university film society. He thought he'd write a piece for the society magazine. After all, he'd practically been in on the death.

Lotte! Ella! Brand closed his eyes. The two women seemed to merge into one and then that one took on another shape and age: a bright little girl at a convent school who couldn't possibly have imagined that more than fifty years later those two other women would die because of her.

He felt suddenly angry. Ella's death was a mistake; but Lotte's was calculated. There was no place for pity in that crime.

'Herr Viertel, I need your help. I don't think Fraülein Bruckner was killed by accident, but deliberately. She knew or thought she knew something relevant to another death and she was coming to you for advice, information. I have to try to find out what that information was. Will you help me?' The rage he felt gave his plea a grating urgency.

Then he saw the man opposite him wince with pain and realized how it must have sounded to him. 'I'm sorry,' he ended lamely.

A flicker of understanding passed across Otto Viertel's wasted features. 'Are you a policeman, Mr Brand?'

'I was. In England. I didn't know it was so obvious.'

'I've been interrogated before,' Viertel said quietly.

'I know. Lotte told me about you. It was inconsiderate of me to barge in on you like this.'

'But you've very little time and time, I know, is precious. Not to me. I'm just living out my time. I was glad when my sight finally failed me. I could no longer see myself as others see me.' He felt for the cup beside him and lifted it to his lips but didn't drink. 'Lotte was very good to me after I returned from America. She'd send me a little money, not that she had much herself. But it helped me find this apartment and set up as a piano teacher. I don't have many pupils. Only the strong ones who can stand the sight of me. What do you want to know, Mr Brand?'

'Does the name Elke Knödel mean anything to you?'

'Oh yes, I remember the girl. I think maybe it was the memory of her that kept me alive in Dachau. Revenge, hate, they're powerful incentives to live. But afterwards it didn't seem to matter. Is she the other dead person you spoke of?'

'No. It was her sister Ella. She hadn't seen Elke or any of her family since she was an adolescent. She'd lived a totally different life. But two days ago she also had what seemed an accident and died.'

'Only you didn't think it was an accident, any more than you believe Lotte was killed accidentally by a hit-and-run driver?' The blind eyes seemed to pierce right through the clutter of doubts that had fogged Brand's mind during the last twenty-four hours.

'I believe Ella was killed by mistake.'

'And Lotte believed that too?'

'I think she did although she wouldn't admit it. I'm convinced she had an inkling of the truth but she refused to say any more until she'd spoken to you. It was after I asked her if there were any other survivors who had known the Hesselmanns and would feel strongly enough to want to murder the girl who'd informed against them.'

'And you thought that might be me, Mr Brand?' There

was a whisper of a chuckle in his voice. 'As you see, it would
have been quite difficult for me.'

'For a moment, yes, I thought that. But now I realize
she wanted your memory to corroborate hers. Was there
someone else?'

Otto Viertel fingered the scar that bisected his cavernous
cheek, as if the ugly wound were a talisman of memory.
'Many of us who worked for the Hesselmanns had reason
to be grateful to them. They were good people, considerate,
generous.'

Brand sensed he was holding back. 'But there was one.
One in particular,' he prompted. 'Herr Viertel, Ella's death
may have been forgivable in a way. Lotte Bruckner's was
cold-blooded.'

'You're right.' He heaved his crippled leg into an easier
position. 'He wasn't much more than a boy. An orphan.
He was part-Jewish. The Hesselmanns took him from the
orphanage and gave him a home. Not as a member of
the family—although Jacob Hesselmann regarded all his
employees as family. But as a gardener's apprentice on the
estate. The boy had a magical aptitude. He was with them
as long as I can recall. He had green fingers and an extraordinary gift for anything mechanical. He created the trick folly
in the Hesselmann grounds. Of course he didn't create it on
his own. It was the work of many craftsmen. But he conceived it. He planned it. A little ornamental garden with
waterfalls, grottos and a wishing-well that had a hidden
secret. Not unlike the trick water garden at Hellbrunn
Palace on a much smaller scale. You know it?'

Brand nodded. 'I know it.'

'The Austrians love their follies, playing jokes on nature.
Forgive me, I'm rambling. It's just remembering. It was all
so beautiful. Then.'

He seemed reluctant to relinquish the memory, clinging
to the image of that golden past his mind's eye was conjuring
up so vividly. And Brand hadn't the heart to jerk him back

to the present, letting him play out his story in his own good time.

'Does the estate still exist intact?'

'Oh yes,' said Otto Viertel. 'It was taken over as a convalescent home for wounded Wehrmacht officers during the war. Then I believe it was acquired as a headquarters by the occupying forces after the war. But by the time I returned to Salzburg it was used to house municipal offices, just outside the town. The gardens are still a showcase open to the public, but you have to have a guide for the folly and the little water garden. It can be quite dangerous if you don't know its secrets.'

'The garden—that was an extraordinary achievement for a young orphan who'd started out as an apprentice gardener.' Brand gently prodded him out of the reminiscences that seemed to give him such comfort. 'What happened to him?'

The crippled man gestured helplessly. 'Who knows? He was one of the casualties of the Nazi round-up of the Hesselmanns. He refused to denounce them publicly, although no one would seriously have blamed him. He was just an employee, a gardener, he could have disappeared into the woodwork like so many. But he didn't. And he was part-Jewish. Like me, he probably ended up in a concentration camp or forced labour group. I never knew. At the time I had my own little problems with the authorities.' His small, twisted smile gave his glancing dismissal of his 'little problems' an added poignancy.

'I don't suppose you remember his name?' Brand held his breath, praying that Otto Viertel's fertile memory would extend that far.

The man shook his head. 'I'm not sure, I'm really not sure. Winter, I believe. Friedrich. Franz, Wilhelm, perhaps. What does it matter? He's almost certainly dead.'

'But supposing he isn't?'

Winter, thought Brand, a common enough German sur-

name as in English, except for the pronunciation. All the
same, it began to make a curious connection in his mind.
He returned his attention to Otto Viertel.

The man shifted his leg again. He looked grey and tired.
The conversation with Brand had exhausted him. 'I can't
tell you any more, Mr Brand.' He passed a weary hand over
his misshapen features. 'I don't wish to be inhospitable
but I'd like you to leave. It's all so long ago. Finished.
Done.'

'But it isn't finished,' said Brand. He despised himself for
prolonging Otto Viertel's anguish, but he still had to find
some key, some link between the past and the two deaths
he was now even more convinced were murder. 'Lotte
Bruckner said something about coming home to roost or
die.'

'Referring to me?' Another twisted smile.

'Perhaps referring to herself. But if this young man, this
gardener, *were* alive today, would *he* come home to roost?'

'Perhaps. For a while when you're finally released from
the hell you've been living through, just trying as best you
can to survive, you want nothing more than to remove
yourself totally from the past. You convince yourself that
you can build a new life and in time forget. But after a while
you realize that a new life doesn't create a new person. In
your mind and your memory you're the same, you can't cut
off your roots. That's why I returned. Maybe, even if they
didn't admit it, that's why Lotte and that woman Ella
returned. Maybe out there is a man, far from young any
more, who remembers the Hesselmanns and the garden he
helped create for them . . .'

'And Elke Knödel.'

'And Elke Knödel,' Otto Viertel admitted. 'Your problem, Mr Brand—a stranger, an Englishman—is finding
him.'

'How would I know him?'

'Maybe you already do, without even realizing it. But

I'm merely indulging your conviction that he's alive. I doubt if he is.'

Maybe I already do, thought Brand, without realizing it. For several seconds he searched the old man's face, but whatever answers he hoped to find there weren't forthcoming.

'Lisa will see you out,' said Otto Viertel. As if she'd been listening behind the door, the little woman bustled in, clattering the coffee cups as she piled them on the tray.

Brand sought Otto Viertel's good hand and was surprised at the firmness of its grip. 'I'm grateful to you.' He paused. 'I was wondering. Elke Knödel. What about her?'

A flicker of surprise crossed Otto Viertel's ravaged face. 'I thought you'd have known. She went to England. For her *services*—' he stressed the word ironically—'to the state she was found a job as nursemaid to the family of a diplomat. A very important man. Carl von Preissing. He was posted as a trade attaché to the German Embassy in London before the war.'

'You've no difficulty in recalling his name.'

'No difficulty at all. In the old days he'd been one of Jacob Hesselmann's good friends. The family were always at the house. Until suddenly it was no longer expedient for them to associate with Jews. But that, as they say, is another story. Isn't it, Mr Brand?'

He inclined his head toward the woman who was waiting, with barely concealed impatience, to usher Brand out of the apartment and out of the leftover life of the man she so devotedly cared for. 'Mr Brand is leaving, Lisa. I don't suppose we'll meet again.'

'But you'll want to know about Lotte Bruckner.'

'What do I need to know? You can't bring her back. You can't bring any of them back. Your justice, Mr Brand. Is it really worth the trouble?'

The question echoed in his ears as he tramped down the winding staircase and into the quiet cobbled street. The woman and the cat were still glaring at him as he passed by the ground-floor window.

CHAPTER 16

Leo Kiesler was unavailable when Brand called at the police station on his way back to the hotel and the sergeant on duty wasn't much help either. His stilted English was adequate for the guarded information he was prepared to pass on. So far as he knew, Inspector Kiesler was aware that Lotte Bruckner had been killed in a car accident. Apparently she'd been knocked down in the street and died almost instantly. And, no, he wasn't empowered to give out any further information unless Brand was a relative, in which case he should go to the hospital where they'd taken her body. The police, naturally, were doing all they could to apprehend the driver of the car. Then he muttered something in German under his breath which, roughly translated, Brand took to be a personal belief that it was probably some hare-brained kid who didn't know the one-way system.

Then he fixed Brand with a beady eye and told him that if he were anything to do with the Press there would be a statement in due course, thus terminating any further discussion.

As he toyed with a sandwich and a stein of lager in a near-by café, Brand tried to fight off the familiar feeling of depression when every explored avenue seemed to lead to a dead end. He recognized from past experience that he'd reached the point where patient investigation wasn't enough. It was time for that lucky break, that flash of instinct unsupported by fact, and he was angry with himself for seeming incapable of summoning up the sudden insight into an impenetratable mystery which had served him so well before. He took out his pipe, filled it with tobacco and lit it, ignoring the distasteful glances of non-smokers around him. But there was no solace in that either. Was he, as Leo Kiesler obviously believed, careering up a blind alley? Why couldn't he accept the simple solution that Armstrong had killed his wife in a rage, that Lotte Bruckner was the victim of a hit-and-run driver?

He re-ran in his mind his conversation with Otto Viertel, searching for clues. But he kept coming back to the blind man's final remark: 'is it really worth the trouble?' It would be the easy way out. After all, it was none of his business. Kiesler was a thoroughly efficient detective. He knew his own patch far better than Brand did.

But then he remembered Ella Armstrong and the strange fear she couldn't explain or understand.

'Yes, by God, it *is* worth the trouble.' The non-smoking group at the next table turned curious, embarrassed faces towards him and he realized he'd spoken his conviction out loud. He heard them whispering among themselves as he left.

By the time he'd returned to the Mariahof he'd recovered some of his resolute conviction that the lucky break he was looking for would be forthcoming. What had Otto Viertel said? Something about knowing the answer without even realizing it. And, quite without prompting, the scene when he'd discovered Ella Armstrong's body in the bath flashed into his mind and with it the nagging feeling he'd had of something quite trivial that was out of true.

If he'd hoped for a quiet session alone with his thoughts he soon realized that any such hope was out of the question. The crowded hotel lobby seemed to be teaming with as much tension as there were people to generate it.

As he let himself through the swing door he bumped into Debbie Price who was standing uncomfortably on the fringe of what appeared to be a major row involving Jake Schneider and a dynamic little man flanked by an entourage of sleek yes-men. The 'heavy mob' from New York of which

Schneider had spoken earlier had obviously arrived.

'Why can't we sleep on it, Louis? Tomorrow is Sunday, rest day. We can work something out,' Schneider was saying helplessly. 'We've got some good stuff. You've seen the rushes. We have to think of the production.'

The dynamo from New York looked at him pityingly. 'Schneider, you don't *have* a production. Your leading man is probably going to be charged with murdering his wife any minute, Judy Clay wants to pull out. And the best thing in the picture, so you tell me, Lotte Bruckner, has been killed by a hit-and-run driver.' He flicked his hard eyes round the Mariahof lobby. 'And what the hell are we doing anyway, staying in a crummy hick hotel like this?'

Brand noticed Fritz wince as he overheard the slighting comment from behind the reception desk in the corner, but he had his problems too. An American guest was loudly complaining to him and the worried manager about a hired car he'd ordered that hadn't arrived. 'I specifically said this evening and it wasn't there in the garage.' The salty voice had a Mississippi twang which seemed to be vying with the other, flatter, meaner voice for attention.

Debbie Price raised pained eyebrows at Brand. She seemed glad to see him.

'Who's that?' said Brand, nodding in the direction of the stocky man with Schneider. His face looked like a scuffed leather shoe that had kicked around too long and his voice sounded as if it had been minced through a meat grinder.

'Officially he's Vice President in charge of international production. Unofficially he's the corporation hatchet man. Louis Wilder. He wants to pull the plug on the movie.' She looked uncharacteristically lost and unsure of herself and Brand realized she wasn't alone. Sundry other member of the unit, still in a state of shock after hearing the news of Lotte Bruckner's death, were clustered in corners of the lobby, looking worried, as if their futures were being decided, which in a sense they were.

'You'd think they'd have the decency to argue it out in private,' she said bitterly.

'I suppose he has a point,' said Brand reasonably.

'Oh, he's got a lot of points, all right. You just heard them. But that's no comfort to us.'

'What happens if he does shut down the production?'

'Two weeks' pay for the crew—and a pay-off for the key members of the unit and cast. Whatever the terms of their contract. Everybody loses, except the company. They'll write off the money already spent on the movie as a tax loss. It's bloody, however you look at it.'

Jake Schneider had lost all his smooth ebullience. He seemed visibly to have shrunk in size over the past two days. The squint in his eye was more pronounced as he passed a shaking hand over his forehead.

'Lou, let's discuss it upstairs,' he said nervously, aware that the row between them was becoming too public for comfort.

Wilder nodded at his henchmen. 'OK. But there's nothing to discuss. Better to cut our losses now. And don't call me Lou.' It was the final insult. Wilder's short legs covered the carpeted floor to the lift with surprising speed. Schneider and the other men pattered after him like puppy dogs in the wake of a masterful mastiff.

Debbie Price's eyes searched the lobby for Fred Hubble and the stills photographer who exchanged hopeless glances with her. She turned to Brand. 'I'm going to get quietly smashed,' she said with a wry smile. 'You can join us if you like.'

Brand shook his head. 'I'll pass, thanks.' He didn't add, 'it's your funeral, not mine,' although it was the truth. But she caught his drift.

'Perhaps you're right. We wouldn't be great company tonight.'

'Where's Matthew?'

She frowned momentarily. In the concern over shutting

down the movie so prophetically titled she'd briefly forgotten the cause of it. 'He's not too bad, I think. Considering. His agent Allan Pennington is holding his hand. What a bloody mess it all is! And to think I turned down a movie for David Puttnam for this one. I thought Salzburg would be more fun than the jungles of Borneo or wherever. Ah well, you win some, you lose some.' And she wandered off arm-in-arm with Fred Hubble.

The argument over the missing hired car was still going on as the dejected members of *The Sound of Murder* unit retired to the bar to drown their sorrows.

'I can't understand what the problem is, sir. The car keys are here at the desk, just as you directed. The car—a Volkswagen Golf, which is what you requested—is in the garage. I've checked myself.' The plaintive note in the manager's voice was coupled with a gesture of the hands which could be taken for supplication or exasperation, depending on how you preferred to interpret it. The guest, feeling himself the injured party, assumed he was being placated and seemed slightly mollified.

'Well, it wasn't there earlier—or the keys. The only Volkswagen on the parking lot was a clapped-out beetle,' he grumbled. But his anger had run its course.

Spotting the hopeful sign, the manager beamed warmly and held out the car keys. 'I'm sure it was just a simple mistake, sir. Our head porter was here all evening . . .' He nodded towards Fritz. 'He'd certainly have reported anything irregular. I'm so sorry you've been inconvenienced.'

Grudgingly the American accepted the apology along with the car keys; the suspicion that the management had somehow come out of the situation with more dignity than he had showed on his face.

For some reason Brand found himself eavesdropping on the petty dispute with increasing interest. Perhaps because it all sounded so normal. Nothing else at the moment came within Brand's definition of normality. Since he'd arrived in Salzburg he seemed to have been living in an unreal world, as unreal as the fiction Jake Schneider and the film crew had been trying to produce on the screen. And the division between the two became more and more blurred. The deaths of Ella Armstrong and Lotte Bruckner were no more bizarre than the fracas in the lobby over the movie's future and the menace engendered by the hatchet man from New York.

There was something almost soothing in listening to a man arguing over such an ordinary . . . ! Only it wasn't quite ordinary. Brand clapped his hand to his forehead. Fool! The tingle of excitement he suddenly felt was so strong that he was sure it must be visible. Deliberately he assumed an expression of calm disinterest as he strolled over to the desk and asked for his room key.

'Trouble?' He smiled at Fritz solicitously.

The man shrugged his shoulders lightly as if to indicate that it was merely one of the routine problems of a head porter adept at dealing with the demands of fractious guests.

'Just a misunderstanding,' he said. As he reached for the key the sleeve of his green jacket rode up his arm. Hastily he pulled it down over his wrist as if he'd committed a sartorial sin.

Brand's eyes met his blandly. 'I've just heard about Fraülein Bruckner. I can hardly believe it.'

'A tragedy, Herr Brand. She was—' the man paused, summoning up the right words—'she was a great lady.' His voice was unsteady.

'A tragedy,' Brand agreed. He nodded towards the bar. 'It looks as if it'll be a heavy night.'

The head porter didn't seem to hear him.

He walked purposefully towards the stairs, but when he reached the first landing he turned down the corridor searching for a service exit. Looking round to make sure he was unobserved, he located the exit, slipped through the door and down the stone stairs past the laundry bins to the back of the hotel. The Mariahof garage was reached by another narrower flight of steps underneath the main structure.

It was dimly lit by naked bulbs at the far corners of the enclosure. There was space for two dozen cars, no more, each space neatly marked with white painted guidelines. It was half empty and the cars, in the unnatural shadowy light, took on the weird disparate shapes of mechanical monsters waiting to be cast in a horror movie.

His ear caught the sound of a faint scuffle and he swung round rapidly. But it was only a mouse interrupted in its search for tasty garbage. He breathed deeply trying to regulate the pound of his heartbeat. I'm getting too old for this kind of thing, he thought. But there was no threat here. Just a collection of inanimate cars.

Meticulously he searched the garage, spotting the 'clapped-out beetle' incongruously sitting beside a spruce new Japanese Subaru. The Volkswagen Golf, brilliantly red, was parked at the rear of the garage just as the hotel manager had assured his irate guest. It was the only Golf there and bore the legend of the hire company on the rear windscreen.

Taking out his pocket torch, Brand flashed the beam round the car until he found what he was looking for. Underneath the front bumper there was a deep indentation. It could have been caused by a slight collision with under car but the torch beam revealed no alien paint marks. Unless all his instincts had played him false, Brand felt sure this was the car that had careered into Lotte Bruckner on that narrow street leading to Otto Viertel's apartment house. Kiesler's forensic experts could ascertain that, he decided. But whether they could also ascertain who had driven it wouldn't be so easy. Whoever had steered the car into Lotte Bruckner had had to make a sudden decision. But Brand judged he'd been a cautious man: someone who had schooled himself over the years to act quickly but not rashly.

He turned off the torch and was about to leave when he felt his foot nudge something soft on the ground beside the driver's door of the Golf. He bent down and picked up what appeared to be an old petrol-stained rag. But as he turned it over something else fell to the concrete floor.

The light-bulb in the ceiling above glittered down on it. It was a soiled white chamois leather glove. He studied it for a moment, then pocketed it. As he did so he heard the measured tread of footsteps behind him, unhurried, as if they knew very well where they were heading.

He braced himself against the prickle of fear that threaded down his spine, wishing he were twenty years younger and fitter. Then he spun round and found himself staring into the curious eyes of the hotel manager.

'Herr Brand. I didn't know anyone was here.' He seemed uncertain whether to apologize for his presence or to demand to know what Brand was doing there.

With a carefully calculated show of relief designed to conceal the real purpose of his inspection of the garage, Brand gasped. 'You surprised me. I came through the garage into the hotel earlier today and thought I must have dropped my wallet. I missed it. But it isn't here.'

'You should have reported it to the desk, Herr Brand.'

Brand waved the suggestion aside. 'I'm sure there's no need. I'll probably find it in my room. I'll let you know if I don't.'

The manager didn't seem too perturbed about Brand's missing wallet. He was a man who didn't wear his worries lightly. And a missing wallet which would almost certainly turn up was the least of them.

'I was just checking on Herr Brindle's car.' He assumed Brand knew all about the American's hired car and didn't much care if he didn't. 'So much trouble. The film unit. Mrs Armstrong's death. Now that awful business of Fraülein Bruckner. It's very disturbing for all of us. All the guests,' he corrected himself.

'You're fortunate in having someone as reliable as Fritz Sommer on the desk. Never leaves his post.'

The man looked so distracted that Brand doubted whether he'd attach any significance to the casual compliment on his choice of staff.

'Fritz? Oh yes, he's very reliable. A tower of strength. I suppose it will all sort itself out in time. But—things like this—they give a hotel a bad reputation.'

'Did he suffer very badly?'

The man dragged his thoughts away from his immediate concerns unwillingly. 'Suffer?'

'In the concentration camp.'

The manager stiffened. 'I don't know what you mean, Herr Brand.'

'I noticed the tattoo on Fritz Sommer's wrist. The number. I assumed he'd been a prisoner.'

'Yes, yes, I see. That was a long time ago. He doesn't speak of it.' He dismissed the subject too casually. 'You will let us know about the wallet, Herr Brand.'

'I promise. But now I come to think of it, the last time I took it out was in Inspector Kiesler's office,' he lied.

'Inspector Kiesler!'

'He's an old friend. He's really the reason why I came to Salzburg.'

The manager drew himself to attention. 'I hope Inspector Kiesler isn't—concerned—about anything to do with the hotel,' he prompted.

'Not that I know of,' Brand said reassuringly. He shivered. 'It's cold down here. I think I'll call it a night.'

'Very wise, Herr Brand.' Brand couldn't be sure whether there was the suggestion of a threat in the manager's voice.

'By the way you've got visitors down here.'

'Visitors?'

'Mice.'

'Mice!' the manager repeated evenly. 'Mice, Herr Brand, we can deal with.'

CHAPTER 17

Judging by the sounds of merriment floating through the door to the bar the mourners lamenting the imminent demise of *The Sound of Murder* had reached that happy state of inebriation in which the only way to confront disaster is to laugh at it. Brand couldn't blame them, but he passed by quickly as Debbie Price caught his eye through the open door. He didn't want to get embroiled in that drama. But there seemed to be no escaping it.

'Mr Brand!' He walked ahead, determinedly trying to appear as if he hadn't heard. 'Mr Brand!' There was no ignoring the more insistent tone.

Debbie Price was standing in the door, looking flushed but far from being 'smashed' as she'd intended.

He turned and sighed. He'd far more urgent matters to attend to and the prospect of listening to the film unit dissecting the bones of a movie that would never reach the screen seemed not only time-wasting but unappealing.

'Look, Miss Price, I'm sorry about the film, but I'm tired and I don't want to intrude on a private party, so . . .'

He must have sounded angry because she looked at him with a hurt expression on her face. 'Sod the film! I just thought you'd want to hear something I forgot to tell you. But, of course, if you can't be bothered . . .' She shrugged a stray lock of hair out of her eyes and turned huffily towards the bar.

'Debbie!' A voice from inside called.

'Coming.'

'No, wait.' Brand called her back. 'I apologize. It's just . . .' He gestured towards the noisy bar.

'Not seemly, I suppose you're going to say.' There was a cynical bite in her voice.

'Something like that,' he admitted.

'Just because we don't sit around weeping and wailing you think we don't care. And I don't mean about losing our jobs. After all, it's just a movie. There'll be others. But you actually believe we don't give a damn that Matthew Armstrong is in an almighty fix, that his wife and Lotte Bruckner are dead. Well, you're wrong, Mr Brand, we care more than you think.'

He felt suddenly contrite and a little silly. What right had he to accuse them of insensitivity because they didn't wear grave faces and talk in hushed whispers? 'You're right,' he said gently. 'What is it you wanted to tell me?'

She accepted his apology with grudging grace. 'I didn't know whether it was important and frankly it slipped clear out of my mind when that awful man Wilder arrived. I was in the lobby with Jake earlier this evening as Lotte Bruckner was leaving the hotel. She seemed pretty agitated, as if she'd got a lot on her mind. When she saw me she called me over and asked me to give you a message. She didn't make a big thing of it, just in passing if I saw you. She thought she'd been a bit abrupt with you and that you weren't to worry.'

'Just that?'

'No, there was something else. But it didn't make much sense. Something about a garden. And summertime. But she'd be more certain later.'

'A garden or a gardener?'

She frowned, trying to remember, then shrugged. 'Honestly, that's all I can recall. As I said, she wasn't making much sense. It was as if she were talking out her thoughts, not really communicating. And she was in a hurry. Then half an hour later we heard she'd been killed by that car or whatever. Louis Wilder arrived and that put the cap on the film. And for a while I couldn't think of anything else.'

She looked at him curiously as Brand digested the garbled

message she'd delivered. If only Lotte had told him this before, she might not now be dead.

'Mr Brand, are you all right?' she said anxiously. 'I know it sounds crazy and it probably doesn't mean anything.'

'On the contrary, it means a great deal.' How could he tell her, if indeed she'd understand, that she'd provided the final piece of the jigsaw puzzle? In any case, it was better that she didn't know. Someone who'd killed twice was capable of killing a third time to protect his secret.

'Miss Price . . .'

'For Pete's sake, call me Debbie. Everyone else does.'

'Debbie. There's one thing you can do for me. But keep it to yourself. I mean that. In the production office you must have lots of maps and brochures of Salzburg, histories of places of interest, possible locations.'

'Of course, that's all part of pre-production. That's Murray Pick, the location manager's, province.'

'Could we go upstairs and look them out for me?'

'Anywhere special?'

He took her arm and hurried her upstairs so that they wouldn't be overheard. She produced a key to the production office and only when he'd closed the door behind him in the deserted room did she repeat her question.

'There are some municipal offices just outside Salzburg laid out in gardens, open to the public for guided tours,' said Brand.

'That's not much to go on.'

'But this may be. The estate used to belong before the war to a Jewish family called the Hesselmanns. It should be easy to locate. It was quite famous. But I'm interested in the layout of the place.'

'Why all the mystery?'

'Debbie, please, just try to find it for me.'

She looked puzzled but opened the filing cabinet and extracted a wadge of maps and brochures.

She laid them out on the desk and he leafed through them,

painstakingly discarding the obvious tourist guides which omitted much reference to the immediate pre-war period with all its painful memories.

'Is this what you're looking for?'

She held up a plain buff folder which had an official stamp on it, the kind you find in town surveyors' departments.

'How did you come by this?'

'The local authorities were very helpful when Jake was scouting locations with the production designer. They looked at dozens of places.'

'And Murray Pick was with them?'

'Not necessarily. He's more concerned with the nuts and bolts of location work, transportation, stuff like that.'

'But this one was never used—or, rather, never scheduled to be used?'

She shook her head. 'Apparently not. See.' She pointed to a note clipped to the file. 'Municipal offices, formerly home of Hesselmann family. Not practicable. Ornamental garden only interest. But difficult access. Denied permission due to possible irreparable damage.' The note was initialled M.P. with a comically sketched skull and crossbones.

'This would have had to be returned to the appropriate authorities?'

'Naturally, it'll go back. It's on loan. But without Murray's little note, I hasten to add.' She gave him a half-smile, both amused and disturbed by the skull and crossbones. 'What do you think that means?'

Brand opened the file and spread out a photocopied map of the house and gardens in front of him. 'It means, I think, that the garden is a trap. A trick garden. With hidden waterfalls and wells that are operated mechanically. You have to know where the gadgets are to make them work. Can I borrow this tonight? I promise I'll return it.'

She lifted her shoulders in a gesture of resignation. 'I don't suppose it matters now.'

Without taking his eyes off the blueprint, Brand thanked

her absent-mindedly. 'You don't know what a help you've been.'

'You're so right. I don't know. I can't begin to guess what this is all about.'

When he didn't reply, she tapped him on the shoulder. 'Will it help Matt?'

He turned towards her and the compassion in her eyes shamed him. In the exhilaration of fitting the bits and pieces of evidence into the pattern of his suspicion, he'd been guilty of playing the game for its own sake, losing sight of the reason for playing it. Debbie Price's touching concern for Matthew Armstrong pulled him up sharply.

'I hope so. I hope it will help him,' he assured her gently. 'Now, go back downstairs, say you've been powdering your nose or something. And remember. This is strictly between us. Promise!'

'You sound so serious. Like my father. It's frightening.' She attempted a frivolous tone, but it rang false, as if she were uncertain whether to take his warning at face value or with a pinch of salt.

'I am serious,' he urged.

She held up her hands in mock capitulation. 'Promise, promise!'

After she'd locked the door behind them, she looked at him dubiously. 'I can't make you out,' she said. 'You seemed . . .'

'. . . an old codger?'

She screwed up her nose, half agreeing with him but too polite to admit it out loud. 'What's the percentage in all this for you?'

'Percentage?'

'I mean, what are you getting out of it? You didn't *have* to get involved with Matt or Ella or Lotte Bruckner and what happened to them, quite apart from whatever it is you're up to now.'

'Let's just say it's the habit of a lifetime.'

She shook her head, still too young to envisage a lifetime, let alone a habit that could consume it.

'Mr Brand,' she said in a small voice, 'are you worried something—something might happen to me?'

'Of course not,' he replied over-heartily. The last thing he wanted was to alarm her. Alarm betrays itself. But simple caution can be contained. 'I only said don't talk about Lotte Bruckner's message—and this—' he gestured with the folder in his hand—'because it's better no one else should know, just yet.'

He was rewarded with a disbelieving smirk. 'Now you really do sound like my father. I wasn't born yesterday, you know. All right, I'll keep your secrets. Old codger!'

He watched her walking jauntily down the corridor, hands in her jeans pockets, and wished he'd handled the situation better. The only protection he could offer her now was speed.

When he reached his room, Brand removed his wallet from his breast pocket and phoned the hotel manager to assure him it had been found. That white lie was a diversion he could do without. Then he fortified himself with a large whisky and mapped out his plan of action.

He took out the soiled white glove he'd found on the floor of the garage and placed it on the bureau along with the map of the old Hesselmann estate. Then he stretched himself fully clothed on his bed and played with a thought he'd shelved at the back of his mind.

The killing of Ella Armstrong had been precise, only chance had prevented it from being an almost perfect murder. He'd never believed in the theory of completely perfect murders, only in the certainty that they'd been imperfectly investigated.

But there was an element of panic in the repeat performance which had resulted in Lotte Bruckner's death. There was no guarantee that she'd have died instantly in that moment when the car drove into her. She could have suffered

severe injuries but survived. Someone could have witnessed
the supposed accident and identified the car. The action
must have been a sudden, necessary impulse. Perhaps death
hadn't even been the intention. Perhaps Ella Armstrong's
killer had merely wanted to scare her.

Whatever the reason, he was convinced it must have
thrown the man he was looking for off balance. Now he'd
be watching, waiting for alarm signals and, hopefully, he'd
respond to them as Brand intended. But he'd need help and
it would take a lot of persuading to make Leo Kiesler agree
to give it.

He picked up the phone and called Kiesler at home. From
the sound of his sleepy voice he was obviously about to turn
in for the night.

'Do you know what time it is, Ralph?' he complained.

Brand looked at his watch. It was after midnight. Over
the last few days time seemed to have been ordered not by
hours but by circumstances.

'I'm supposed to be taking the family to early Mass
tomorrow,' the inspector grumbled.

'Leo, I know this is an imposition. But please hear me
out.'

Maybe it was the urgency in Brand's voice or the desire
to get shot of the unwelcome midnight call, but Kiesler
listened patiently as Brand talked for several minutes, ending finally: 'Will you do this for me, Leo? It's the only way.'

'It's highly irregular, Ralph.'

Brand sighed. How often had he heard that argument
from his own superiors in the past!

'But what have you got to lose, Leo? A couple of phone
calls and . . .'

'And what if it doesn't work? More important, what if it
does work? Do you realize the danger you're putting yourself
in? If—and I'm still not convinced—if your suspicion is
correct.'

'Leo, there's always a risk.' Now that he'd hooked Kiesler

he could afford to make light of it. 'And you know what they always say: if curiosity killed the cat it can also catch a killer.'

'I never heard that.'

'Well, you have now.'

'I suppose it's occurred to you that someone might be listening in to this call?'

'That's a chance I had to take. It would have looked more peculiar if I'd left the hotel and made the call from a public telephone!

'Well, just watch it, Ralph. I don't want to have to send you back to England in a box.'

'Don't worry, Leo. I'm very good at watching out for myself. Well, most of the time,' he admitted.

His next long-distance call to England provoked an even louder explosion from the other end and another demand to know whether he realized what time it was.

His former colleague on the police force, Inspector John Waller, had been watching a late-night movie on Television and Brand had interrupted him at a moment of high, crucial drama.

'You've seen *The Big Sleep* a dozen times before, Waller. If you don't remember I'll tell you how it comes out in the end. Humphrey Bogart and Lauren Bacall—'

'Ralph, have you been drinking?' said Waller suspiciously.

'Yes. I've a large Scotch beside me. But I'm not drunk and I do need your help. A favour.'

'What is it? And why at this time of night?'

'That's better.'

After Brand had finished talking, he heard Waller sigh heavily. 'You're not asking much, are you? Quite apart from the fact that you've no longer any authority to ask for or receive this information. Not unless you go through normal civilian channels.'

It was Brand's turn to sigh. 'I know I haven't the authority, Waller. But you have and who's it going to harm?'

'But, good Lord, it's Sunday tomorrow. Today.'

'Come on, Waller. Scotland Yard never sleeps. All they've got to do is run up the past records on a computer. There has to be a file somewhere. All the staff of the German Embassy were under surveillance then. But it's not as if it's top secret information I'm asking for.'

'You want to bet? Everything's top secret these days. They won't even give you Margaret Thatcher's maiden name without a password.'

'Oh, stop griping, Waller. You've got your sources. Say you'll give it a try.'

'All right, I'll see what I can do,' he agreed grudgingly. 'But don't count on it. They're going to think it a pretty funny request anyway. Damn!'

'Damn what?'

'I've missed it. The end. This is going to cost you a couple of pints when you get back to England. Now be quiet and buzz off—Brand.' Needling his former boss was one of Waller's small pleasures which in no way undermined the genuine affection and regard they both retained for each other.

'Thanks, Waller. I'll make it a magnum of champagne.'

'On your pension? Fat chance! By the way—have a nice holiday. What's left of it.'

As he put down the phone, Brand heard the members of the film unit weaving their way along the corridors to their rooms. The lift doors clanged, voices were raised and then hastily hushed into penetrating whispers punctuated by peals of laughter greeting the odd derisory reference to *The Sound of Murder* biting the dust.

He brushed his teeth, slipped into his pyjamas and slid gratefully under the bedcovers. He felt calm and ready for sleep. Tomorrow he'd have to be on his mettle as he'd never been before and he relished the prospect. Tomorrow, he hoped, he would finally lay the ghosts of Ella Armstrong and Lotte Bruckner and a silly, malicious servant girl named Elke Knödel whose action fifty years before spanned the decades, adding two more lives to the others she'd condemned to death in Dachau.

CHAPTER 18

Brand awoke to the sound of church bells which complemented the mellow stillness of a sunny Sunday morning. He allowed himself the luxury of breakfast in bed, collecting his thoughts, before galvanizing himself into action. His plan depended on exact timing. 'But what if it doesn't work?' Kiesler had said. As he sliced the lather from his face with even strokes of his razor he considered the question. The night before he'd been so sure. Now he realized how much he was relying on the vagaries of chance. Kiesler had understood that immediately.

He wiped off the remains of the lather with a towel and faced himself in the mirror, studying the weathered contours, the crevasses of age lining his cheeks, the folds of flesh under his chin, as if seeing himself for the first time. You're growing old, Brand, he thought. And he wondered whether his brain was suffering the same ageing process. Am I indulging in an old man's ego-trip, convincing myself that I'm still as sharp and alert as I was twenty years ago?

Then he remembered standing in this same spot in his bathroom two days before and he heard her voice 'Brand! *Warum?*' as clearly as he'd heard it before she'd died, like a reproachful tape-recorder that refused to be switched off until he'd done what he'd set out to do. 'Damn it, the worst I can do is make a fool of myself,' he said angrily, out loud, to the face in the mirror, daring it to give him an argument.

Emptying the coffee-pot into his cup, he glanced at the

map he'd borrowed from Debbie Price the night before, pocketed it safely and finished dressing.

Downstairs, a slumbrous, morning-after atmosphere permeated the lobby of the Mariahof and the distant purr of a vaccuum cleaner sounded like a lullaby.

There was no sign of the film unit who were obviously taking full advantage of their rest day in bed and contemplating the prospect of 'resting' a good deal longer if New York carried out its threat to close down the picture. The other hotel guests had either made an early start or were taking a breather from strenuous sightseeing. Everywhere in the world, it seemed, Sunday had its own special ambience.

But at the desk, Brand noted thankfully, Fritz, correct and formal in his uniform, was on duty as usual. He seemed to work on automatic pilot during the tourist season, never showing signs of fatigue.

'You're up early, Herr Brand,' he greeted him.

'I've a long day planned,' said Brand, composing his words and his expression with care.

He detected a flicker of interest behind that impersonal mask. 'By the way, Fritz, I found this in the garage last night. I thought it might belong to you.' He withdrew the grubby white chamois leather glove from his jacket pocket.

The head porter looked at it quickly, then turned disdainful eyes towards Brand. 'No, sir, it's not mine. As you see, I wear cotton gloves.' He held up his habitually gloved hand. 'They're easier to launder. But if you leave it with me I'll see if it belongs to one of the guests who may have dropped it when parking a car.'

He made to take the glove but Brand returned it to his pocket. 'Don't worry, Fritz. I'll find the owner.' He wondered what was going on behind those imperturbable eyes, but the head porter gave him no clue.

'Fritz, could you do something for me?' He leaned across the desk confidentially.

'Of course, sir, if I can.'

'I'm going out to the Hesselmann estate this morning.'
He paused, allowing the information time to sink in while
at the same time not appearing to give too much weight to
it.

This time he got the reaction he was waiting for. 'But the
Hesselmanns . . .' Fritz pulled himself up sharply, then
continued blandly. 'I don't know of any Hesselmann estate,
sir, in or around Salzburg.'

'No, that's right,' Brand went on, as if addressing himself
to his memory rather than to the man behind the desk. 'Otto
Viertel told me about it last night. It was taken over by the
municipality as offices after the war. I understand there's a
splendid ornamental water garden in the grounds.'

The head porter seemed unimpressed, paying polite attention, but with half an eye on the guest who'd materialized
beside Brand demanding postage stamps. 'Excuse me, Herr
Brand.'

'Of course, Fritz. I'm taking up your time.'

Pretending an interest in the revolving display of postcards, Brand watched the man out of the corner of his eye
as he dealt speedily and courteously with the other guest.
He'd achieved one small crack in his composure, one hint
of something approaching emotion. But the recovery had
been instant. What personal experiences had combined
to create those granite defences! What experiences had
generated the need for such defences!

'Herr Brand!'

He returned a gaudy view of the Hohensalzburg to the
display stand and turned back to the desk.

'I recall the place you mean now. The estate did once
belong to a family, I believe.'

'Tragic, I understand.' Brand searched the man's face
keenly for some response as he condensed the story he'd
been told by Lotte Bruckner and Otto Viertel. 'The family
ended up in a concentration camp all on the word of an
informant. And none of them survived.'

'Indeed!' The head porter sounded as if it were the first he'd heard of it.

'Ah well, that was a long time ago, wastn't it, Fritz?'

The man's cool eyes betrayed nothing, no remorse for or even acknowledgement of the past. 'What was it you wished me to do, Herr Brand?' he said with the merest touch of impatience. 'I understand the municipal garden is closed to the public on Sundays. It would be a pity to have a wasted journey.'

'Oh, I don't think that will be a problem. I've a special reason for wanting to go there.' Brand lowered his voice. 'I'm expecting a call from Inspector Kiesler shortly. Would you be sure to tell him where I am. I haven't had a chance to speak to him and it's important.'

'Of course, sir. I'll see he gets the message.'

'And Fritz, if anyone else asks for me—any one from the film unit—I'd rather they didn't know where I am. I can rely on you, can't I?'

He took out his wallet ostentatiously.

The head porter looked affronted. 'There's no need for that, Herr Brand. You can rely on me.'

There was a trace of smiling superiority in his expression as he watched Brand sheepishly pocket his wallet. It was the expression of a man who'd won a trifling game of one-upmanship.

He's got my measure, thought Brand, with satisfaction.

He glanced at the clock on the wall behind the desk. Ten o'clock. He had two hours. If his reckoning were correct, two hours should be sufficient.

His heart sank as he heard two wrangling voices behind him.

'Schneider, that's final. Cut. The end. I'm calling New York this morning.'

'But Lou!'

The argument over the future of *The Sound of Murder* had apparently reached the point of no return. Louis Wilder, the hatchet man from head office, sounded as implacable as he had the night before. It had obviously been a fruitless night for the producer Jake Schneider.

Brand made for the swing doors of the Mariahof hastily, ignoring Schneider's call as he spotted him. 'Brand! I've got to talk to you. Matt needs your help, he's asking for you. Brand . . .' His voice trailed away lamely, seemingly torn between the plight of his leading man who wasn't likely to be a leading man much longer and the far more pressing need to make a last-ditch attempt to save his picture.

As he plunged through the door, Brand heard with gratification the soothing tones of the head porter presumably in answer to Schneider's query. 'I'm so sorry, Herr Schneider. He didn't say where he was going.'

Then he caught Wilder's gravelly voice which despite its low pitch had the carrying quality of a tenor's high C. 'What's with this old cop? Armstrong's a dead duck so far as we're concerned. Just get out those redundancy notices. I've a plane to catch. And another thing . . .'

Whatever the other thing might have been was lost to Brand as he paused to draw breath on the pavement outside the Mariahof, relieved that he'd managed to avoid being sidetracked by Schneider or Matthew Armstrong's problems. That would have scuppered all his plans.

'It's a nice morning, Herr Brand.'

Brand gave a start. The hotel manager had emerged from the back entrance to the Mariahof, but Brand had the feeling he'd been waiting for him.

Brand nodded but said nothing.

'A good day for sightseeing. Not so many crowds,' the manager persisted.

'You're right. A good day.' Brand breathed deeply, taking in the sparkling air and facing the sun that was already high in a clear blue sky, as if to reinforce his assertion.

'How much longer will we have the pleasure of your company, Herr Brand?'

The question was innocent enough, but the emphasis behind it caught Brand by surprise. It wasn't a pleasant inquiry, rather a suggestion that his continuing presence wasn't all that welcome.

'I'm not sure. A day, maybe two. It depends.'

'I see. You'll let us know, as soon as possible.'

'I'll let you know.'

The manager smiled curtly and disappeared through the door back into the hotel.

For a moment Brand looked at the closed door, feeling off balance. The encounter had been one of those vagaries of chance he hadn't taken into his calculations. On the face of it the manager's query about his departure could have been merely a polite topic of conversation. But he sensed a deeper concern. Or was he just imagining something that wasn't there?

Despite the warmth of the sun, he shivered. And he wished the day were over. For good or ill, he wished it were over.

Then resolutely he set out through the town and along the footpath by the Salzach river. He'd judged that it would take him forty minutes to walk to the old Hesselmann estate. Forty minutes to prepare himself and enough time for news of his mission to reach the ears of the right person.

Deep in thought, he barely noticed the few idling tourists, the river boats and the excursion coaches whooshing past him to pleasurable destinations in the Tyrol and the Alpine resorts with their White Horse Inns and picture-book family restaurants.

A few of the faces behind the smoked windows of the coaches looked at him oddly, as if aggrieved that he wasn't responding to the sun and the scenery and the serenity as they should be enjoyed. A square, bulky man in tweeds too heavy for the season, his head down, measuring his steps and frowning at the pebbled pavement. Then they forgot him.

The municipal offices signalled their presence well in

advance. They were high on a hill overlooking the river. The mellow sand-coloured family home with its staggered sloping green-tiled roofing seemed to have remained intact through its various incarnations. No careless bureaucratic hands had put their ugly stamp on it. A graceful drive led to a double flight of steps jutting from the front door. Beyond were the gardens. Only a discreet sign at the entrance indicated that it housed the offices of a department of the city administration. It looked, like all offices on a Sunday, shuttered and aloof, locked in with its filing cabinets and desks and empty rooms.

For a while Brand gazed at the house, its rows of long windows like sightless eyes in a face that had learned to mask its true identity. And he felt strongly the pull of the past. As it must have been. When the Hesselmanns gave their parties and tried to ignore the future that was happening so few miles away across the border in Germany.

He heard the bustle and the laughter and the music as clearly as if he'd stepped into a time warp. All gone. And for the first time he questioned what he was about to do. There were all kinds of justice. His was the justice of law and it seemed in that fractional moment a thin excuse.

But then he remembered Lotte Bruckner who had been killed not out of any kind of justice, but out of fear of discovery. And he knew his instincts were right. Whatever the possible danger to himself.

He lowered his head and when he looked up again he saw just a house which had once been a home. Nothing more. The ghosts had evaporated.

He took out the map for one last inspection, then made his way round the side of the house to the entrance to the gardens. A square sign informed him that they were open to the public from 1000 to 1800 hours each week day and closed on Sundays. But the padlock on the gate, as he'd expected, wasn't locked and he let himself through into a gravel courtyard from which semi-circular stone steps fanned out into a wooded park nestling round a small manmade lake, flanked by statues of water nymphs. The waterfalls, which during visiting hours spurted from hidden sources concealed in the paved surrounds, were silent. Only the guides knew where the secret taps were located.

In other circumstances he'd have enjoyed the leisure of admiring the scene. But he'd used up enough precious time and he tramped hurriedly round the lake towards the garden within a garden that had been the triumphant achievement of a young half-Jewish gardener fifty years before.

It was set in the main body of the park reached through a wrought-iron gate, intricately moulded into beguiling patterns. By comparison with the rest of the grounds it was a small enclosure, a diminutive nineteenth-century Disneyland of delight, with figurines of fairytale characters clustered in groups round a circular pond which at the turn of a key would be mechanically animated. The shrubs and flower beds were scaled to the size of the garden and the scent of the blossoms hung heavily in the trapped air. The heat of the sun was now stifling. But Brand was only aware of the cold sweat that damped his palms and his forehead. Overlooking the garden another flight of stone steps led to a grotto. He ducked his head through the low door and found himself in a cool, darkened room. When his eyes became accustomed to the light after the brilliance of the sun outside, he realized it was walled with multi-coloured mosaics.

Fantastical faces beamed from the mosaics with open mouths ready to spray the unwary with water. In the centre was a round grooved surface. As he stepped on it it gave a hollow ring, sinister in that mystical stillness.

The eyes on the carved faces round the walls seemed to be mocking him, their open mouths silently laughing.

He stood there, transfixed, longing to get out into the comforting sunshine and yet powerless to move. He wanted to hear people, the shrieks of visitors suddenly showered with water in fun. But there was no fun here. Nothing but that awesome silence.

He forced himself to look down at his watch, at some practical everyday, useful appliance. But he had trouble focusing in the dim light. It must be midday. I must get a grip on myself, he told himself. But still he couldn't move. The grotto seemed to exercise a spell he couldn't shake.

Then suddenly he knew he wasn't alone.

'It has that effect. My grotto.'

The voice came from the low door and the figure standing in the opening blocked out what little light had penetrated the exotic interior.

CHAPTER 19

As he spun round, Brand misjudged his footing and almost fell. When he recovered himself, he shielded his eyes with the palm of his hand, peering at the shadowy figure obscuring the exit. Framed in the iridescent light from the garden it took on a weird, inhuman shape as if one of the statues outside had somehow animated itself.

Then, as it shifted round, the light caught the face and the figure became real, not a mythical creature but flesh and blood with a recognizable identity. 'You really shouldn't have come here on your own, Herr Brand.'

Fritz Sommer stepped lightly, assuredly, into the grotto, with the confidence of someone who knew its every secret. And in his loden green jacket there was indeed a gnomish quality about him.

Brand's realization that he'd been right after all was tempered by a quickening alarm. Here in this grotto Fritz Sommer was on home ground, the spellbinder not the spell-bound like Brand. If only he could keep that alarm from showing just long enough to find out what needed to be known from the man himself!

'What did you hope to find in this garden?'

The head porter's tone was deceptively agreeable but there was a hint of real anxiety behind the question. The curiosity that Brand had banked on, the flaw that catches the killer. It was enough. He felt more sure of himself, but not so sure that he could afford to make a mistake.

'Evidence of the young man who conceived it,' he replied, choosing his words carefully. 'A gardener who owed everything to the family that had adopted him and never forgave the person who informed against them. Fritz! That's a nickname for Friedrich, isn't it? But you've changed your surname from Winter to Sommer, haven't you? A switch of seasons. Winter—Sommer. Not very original, Fritz, but good enough to obscure your identity. Otto Viertel thought it was something like that, although he couldn't quite remember. But he remembered *you* very clearly.'

It wasn't strictly the truth. Quite obviously Viertel hadn't been aware that Fritz had assumed another surname. The test would be if Fritz believed it.

A flicker of uncertainty came into the impassive eyes and passed as quickly.

'Otto Viertel is blind,' he said.

'But Lotte Bruckner wasn't. She was on her way to see him when she was killed. She thought she recognized you, yesterday evening, but it was the change of name that bothered her and you knew that because you were there. She left a message for me. But the person who delivered it misheard her. She thought she said "summertime". I realize now what Lotte Bruckner actually said was "Sommer". But she still wasn't sure that you were the young gardener she knew as Fritz Winter. That's why she had to have it confirmed by Otto Viertel. Only she didn't get the chance, did she? You made a mistake when you killed Ella Armstrong thinking she was her own sister, Elke. But you thought you'd covered it up very well. An accident! And when the police began to believe that it wasn't an accident, her husband was a handy suspect. He'd been there at the time and he admitted they'd had an argument. You were twice lucky, Fritz. Until I clumsily involved Lotte Bruckner. She was a problem. And still you thought you could get away with it. Except you had to work quickly. And even then you were lucky. You had the keys to the American guest's hired car in the garage. And even if the car had been identified no one would necessarily associate the driver with you. You were just the head porter, part of the hotel furniture. No one ever notices hotel porters.'

Brand studied the man's face for signs of a crack in that impenetratable mask, but he continued to look at Brand coolly. On either side of him the grotesque, clownish faces set in the brilliant mosaic walls assumed a more menacing, protective aspect.

'You have a vivid imagination, Herr Brand. But then you're a policeman. I don't deny I worked for the Hesselmanns. They recognized my skills and they spared no expense in allowing me to realize my dream. For that and much else I loved the family. And I paid the price.'

'I know, Fritz, I spotted the tattooed numbers on your wrist. How many years was it? Where was it? Dachau, Buchenwald, Auschwitz, Treblinka?'

Even as he spoke them the place names gagged in Brand's throat, the itinerary of a monstrous package tour to hell. He felt an appalled sense of shame as he watched their effect on Fritz Sommer. The wary, watchful expression crumbled, the features rearranged themselves into an effigy of anguish too intense to be comprehended by anyone who hadn't shared it. The cool eyes glowed hotly as if stoked by the coals of an inner fire which, damped down for years, had suddenly blazed back into life, giving off no healing warmth, only the white heat of hate.

He clapped his hands over his ears, crushing them tightly

against the sides of his head, the skin, stretched tautly, gave his face the look of a surreal distortion of a human countenance, not unlike the gargoyle faces on the walls of the grotto.

Some of the pain he was inflicting on the man shot through Brand. I've no right, he thought, no right. But he'd gone too far to retreat now.

As if he'd communicated out loud his own distress, he heard Fritz Sommer echo his very thought. 'What right have you?' He'd regained a measure of control over the grim memories Brand had reactivated and he spoke quietly, simply, like a patient schoolmaster trying to explain the inexplicable to a child. 'What right have you, a safe, comfortable Englishman, to imagine you know about those years?'

'No right,' Brand admitted. 'But perhaps I *can* imagine what sustained you through those nightmare years, that someday you might get your revenge on the girl who'd destroyed the Hesselmanns and, in the deepest sense, you too.'

Fritz Sommer's head shot up. 'I? I survived. I survived to carry out the mission.'

'You carried out the mission, Fritz—or so you thought. But did you survive? Did you truly?'

The question in Fritz Sommer's eyes was directed not at Brand but at himself as if his interrogator had touched a raw nerve.

'What happened to your life after you were released from the camp, Fritz?' Brand pressed on. 'What happened to those gifts of yours, the talent and craftmanship that planned all this?' He gestured round the magical grotto and out into the gardens. 'Were they destroyed in the camps, too?'

Almost imperceptibly, the man nodded, acknowledging a truth he perhaps had never cared to admit before. 'I had no spirit for the trivialities of life any more,' he said strangely.

'Is this so trivial? A mechanical water garden that has

given pleasure to people for so long, who marvel at the imagination that planned it?'

'Pleasure!' Fritz Sommer spat out the word as if it had an acrid taste. 'I had no time, no feeling, for pleasure any more. No peace. A poet, a painter, needs to be driven. But this—this—requires a peace of mind. A patient content-ment. For years as a boy and a young man with the Hessel-manns I enjoyed those blessings and used them to help create this haven. It was my offering to them. But then in the camps I lost the capacity for peace and contentment— along with so much else.'

'You could have found them again. Otto Viertel did.'

'I didn't want to find them,' he said bitterly. 'If I had . . .'

'You might have come to terms with the hate that nourished you,' Brand finished for him. 'For forty years you let that hate consume you. But sometimes it must have seemed a vain hope of vengeance. Sometimes you must have wondered whether you'd ever catch up with Elke Knödel, whether indeed she were still alive. And then finally you could hardly believe your luck—if that's the word—when you thought you'd found her. When was it? Sometime before I arrived? Ella was scared that someone was watching her. Or was it that morning when Ella Armstrong and I were booked on *The Sound of Music* excursion and she joked about how her maiden name was Knödel and that she'd been born in a village named Grinzing. You were there, too, Fritz. That morning. You heard it all. But you were just someone behind the desk, blending with the scenery, doing his job, a faceless hotel servant.'

'A faceless hotel servant.' Fritz Sommer repeated with a hint of satisfaction as if he'd been complimented on giving a convincing performance.

'Was that why you returned to Salzburg after the war? In the hope that Elke Knödel would come back, too?'

'I came back because this is my home. When you've suffered six years in a concentration camp, blending into the scenery, as you put it, seems a welcome, a comfortable, refuge. After we were liberated, what was left of us, I spent months in a hospital run by the British where I learned English. I learned well and colloquially. It was a useful attribute for later. When I returned to Salzburg I discovered what had happened to the Hesselmanns. That's when I changed my name. For a while I hoped . . . maybe it would help to blot out the past, but I knew deep down that nothing could ever do that. I tried several trades, anything rather than what I could do best, until I got the job at the Mariahof and I've stayed there ever since.'

'Waiting! How many times have you come to this garden, Fritz, over the years? Planning what you'd do when and if the time came? You had a long, long time to plan. But did it work out as you'd expected? Tell me, Fritz, did it work out?' Even as he pitied the man almost more than he could bear, his police training forced Brand into needling him to the point where his long-nurtured caution would desert him.

His mouth trembled and the eyes that looked at Brand were glazed with guilt. 'I don't regret that woman. She was the wrong one, but she was her blood, her family. But I regret Lotte Bruckner. I didn't want to kill Lotte Bruckner. I don't know . . .' He looked round the grotto abstractedly, as if it had suddenly seemed to him a prison of his own making. 'I don't know if I just wanted to—to stop her. I didn't think she'd die.' There was an imploring note in his voice as if he needed Brand to understand.

'You panicked, Fritz,' said Brand gently. 'In all those years, didn't it ever occur to you that if it came to the point one murder would not be enough?'

At the mention of murder, Brand noticed a subtle transformation in Fritz Sommmer. It was as if they'd been talking at cross purposes. Revenge had the ring of justice in it and it conferred on the killer a cause, even a noble cause, in his own eyes. Murder was the ultimate crime committed by a criminal. And the man suddenly became aware of his new, dangerous status.

'How?' There was no need for him to elucidate.

'How did I know it was you, Fritz? Little things. You always wear your green jacket during the day, but when you came to Ella Armstrong's room with the key after she was murdered you were wearing your black linen jacket, the one you put on at night. Why? Probably because when you pushed her over in the bath, fracturing her skull and holding her under the water the green coat got wet. You just had time to change before Debbie Price called you. And you were wearing white gloves. Not the cotton ones you claimed you always use. But chamois leather gloves, much like the one I found in the garage beside the car after Lotte Bruckner's death. I still have it and it shouldn't be too hard to identify it as yours. And then on that evening you weren't on duty at the desk. I know because your deputy had to stand in for you. He said the manager had called you away, but later the manager assumed you'd been on duty all the time. This is evidence, Fritz. Evidence that can be investigated and confirmed. But there was something else, too. Not hard evidence, but it made me wonder. Before Ella Armstrong died she spoke in German. "*Warum?*" She hardly ever spoke German unless it was necessary. Unless she were asking that question of someone of her own nationality.'

He let the information sink in, sensing the man's brain, like a ferret in a cage, searching for a loophole, an escape hatch. Then his face cleared. He looked at Brand shrewdly.

'But the police don't know this, do they, Herr Brand?'

Carefully, Brand disguised his expression, seemingly caught out in a deliberate bluff.

'And this garden,' he hurried on, as if trying to retrieve his balance of power over Fritz Sommer. 'This garden. There's the evidence here, too. You left your mark, Fritz, although you didn't realize it.'

It was a calculated lie. There was nothing here to implicate Fritz in anything other than its inspired conception. But he didn't give the man the chance to refute it. Instead he played on the alarm he had finally aroused in him.

'Your evidence counts for nothing, Herr Brand, if you're the only one who possesses it.' The menace in the man's voice was unmistakable and again Brand felt the unreasoning shiver of fear that Fritz Sommer knew the secrets of this hidden place far better than he.

'You forget, Fritz, I left a message for Inspector Kiesler.'

The man smiled, a safe, knowing smile. 'Ah yes, the message you left for Inspector Kiesler.' He moved closer to Brand causing the latter to retreat nervously, not sure to which part of the dim grotto he was being manœuvred. 'What a pity about Inspector Kiesler. He did telephone just as you said he would, soon after you left. Only I didn't tell him you had come out to the Hesselmann estate as you said. I explained you'd decided to take an excursion to Innsbruck for the day. He sounded surprised, but not unduly concerned. In fact, he seemed quite pleased for you. He asked me to tell you that he'd telephone later this evening, after you'd returned. So you see, Herr Brand, it's just between you and me, isn't it?'

'You won't get away with it this time, Fritz.' Knowing what he knew, hoping that his own plans hadn't in some way gone awry, Brand still had an uneasy feeling that a false move could forfeit his life. He was under no delusion that the man moving so slowly, so inexorably, towards him, was not capable of killing him.

He strained his ears and thought he heard the faint crunch of a footstep on gravel in the garden outside. But it could have been a whisper of breeze in the shrubbery or maybe he'd just imagined the sound, willing it to be real.

He felt old and sluggish, conscious that his heart was beating too rapidly. Although they were much of an age, Fritz Sommer was sure-footed, his measured movements deceptive. They were both bargaining for their lives but it was an uneven contest. There was no denying who was the stronger man as Fritz Sommer continued to edge forward, forcing Brand to back away.

There was a fanatical note in his voice as he commiserated with his victim. For that, Brand realized, was what he had become. Another victim. 'I'm sorry you too have to die, Herr Brand. If only you hadn't felt compelled to meddle. But before you do die I'd like you to see my garden, my grotto, as it should be seen.'

Never taking his eyes from Brand, he felt behind him, his hand connecting with a disguised panel in the mosaic wall. At first there was just a trickling sound of water. Then from the orifices of the faces round the walls spurted jets of sparkling water, drenching the floors of the grotto, and strange, unidentifiable birdsongs echoed round the cavern. The tinkling, unearthly sound combined with the rush of water contrived a suffocating cacophony. Brand tugged at his collar, gasping for breath.

'You see! You see!' There was a madness in Fritz Sommer's eyes as he surveyed the magic of his craft, so painstakingly constructed all those years ago in his youth. 'You're supposed to enjoy it, to laugh, as all the tourists laugh. Why aren't you laughing, Herr Brand?' he goaded him.

All the time he kept inching forward.

'That's enough, Fritz. You've had your fun.' Recovering his breath, Brand tried to summon up a tone of calm reason.

But Fritz Sommer was beyond any kind of reason. He was obsessed with a perverse pride in his inventions.

'Oh, but you haven't seen my cleverest triumph. Not even the tourists see this. They don't show it. It's too dangerous. It's my very own secret. Even the guides aren't told how to operate it. My wishing-well!' He breathed the words as if they were a benediction. 'Jacob Hesselmann ordered it to be drained and sealed over when a foolhardy guest almost drowned in it. But for you I'll make an exception. You must have a wish, Herr Brand.'

'Fritz, for God's sake . . .'

'Don't speak of God, Herr Brand. He forsook me and the Hesselmanns and millions like us fifty years ago. Watch!'

He circled round Brand swiftly as if goading him to step in the wrong direction. Then he reached behind the fan-like ear of one of the faces on the wall. Brand looked around him helplessly, then down at his sodden feet and he realized he was standing in the centre of the grooved circle he'd noticed earlier.

As Fritz Sommer's hand connected with the hidden switch, he mustered what will he had left to leap out of the mysterious circle. As he sprawled on the drenched floor he watched aghast as the sides of the circle retracted, exposing a yawning gap in the floor of the grotto. The water spurting down on him from the grinning masks on the walls felt like icy needles on his face.

When he saw that Brand had managed to save himself, Fritz Sommer rushed forward. 'You haven't made your wish,' he cried wildly. As he said it, his feet skidded from under him on the slippery wet surface and he plunged into the well, one hand in its white glove clinging to the side.

Brand edged forward, grabbing the hand. With all his strength he tried to maintain the grip, at the same time sensing without really noticing that they were no longer alone in the grotto.

'Hang on, Fritz, hang on,' he begged desperately.

But even as he spoke he felt the hand slipping away from him, leaving the limp white glove clasped in his own. Then he heard a piercing scream echoing down the deep well, bouncing off the walls, ending in a dull, dead thud.

He felt a pair of strong arms haul him to his feet.

'I thought you'd never get here, Leo. You managed to hear all that?'

Kiesler nodded. 'Can you stand all right, Ralph?'

'Just about.'

Leo Kiesler signalled to the young policeman, ordering him to find the park-keeper.

'I'm sorry, Ralph. I left as soon as I telephoned that fake message to Sommer. If we'd come in earlier he might have panicked and really finished you.'

'He damn near did.'

'I know. I told you it was a risk.' He shivered. The birdsongs and rushing water were unnerving him, too. 'Do you know how to turn these things off?'

Brand indicated the location of the water fountain panel and the wishing-well switch.

Kiesler placed a steadying hand under Brand's elbow. 'Well, you were right and I was wrong. You've found your killer, Ralph. You must be proud.' There was, Brand detected, the merest hint of reproach in the compliment.

He looked down at the twisted body of Fritz Sommer sprawled at the bottom of the wishing-well and he felt no sense of triumph.

'I'm not so very proud,' he said.

CHAPTER 20

The funerals of Ella Armstrong and Lotte Bruckner were held on successive days in Salzburg. On both occasions the cast of principal mourners at the respective graveside were identical.

Key members of *The Sound of Murder* film unit led by Jake Schneider paid their respects. Their grief looked genuine, although Brand suspected it was concentrated as much on their current state of unemployment as on the two dead women. Leo Kiesler represented the Salzburg police force and a worried official in sombre black had been deputed to appear for the municipal authority.

Tributes in flowers and messages had poured in from film

communities all over the world for Lotte Bruckner and the young priest spoke of her in glowing terms as a native of Salzburg who had enriched the cinema with her talent. His service for Ella Armstrong was briefer and more restrained.

As the last mourners drifted away at both funerals Otto Viertel, assisted by the protective Lisa, hobbled towards the graves and tossed into each a single white rose.

Brand watched him in silence as he wiped a tear from his sightless eyes. He was about to speak to him but Lisa shook her head fiercely, her eyes plainly saying, 'You've done enough.'

The single white roses seemed to Brand more poignant than all the other lavish floral tributes.

'So, what are your plans now, Ralph?'

Brand roused himself from his contemplation of Otto Viertel's gentle, caring gesture to face Kiesler.

'Back to England. I'll be leaving tomorrow.'

'It hasn't been much of a holiday. But you'll be back, my friend. In time.'

Brand smiled and nodded, avoiding Kiesler's eyes. 'Sometimes, Leo, I get the feeling I'm running out of time. Give my love to Maria and the children.'

Then he punched his friend's arm fondly in farewell and trudged down the gravel path of the cemetery. For some reason, since Fritz Sommer's death they'd run out of the right things to say to each other. On the way he passed Matthew Armstrong, leaning heavily on Allan Pennington, who glanced blankly at Brand as if he'd never seen him before in his life.

So far as the film unit was concerned, Brand was the forgotten man. Only Debbie Price noticed him as she hurried through the hotel corridor in the throes of packing up the production office.

'It's been nice knowing you, Mr Brand.' She looked harassed but also a shade guilty. 'It's all been so chaotic,' she said hesitantly, 'but really we are grateful for what you've done. For Matthew. And everything,' she ended lamely. 'I suppose you're some sort of hero.'

'Not noticeably,' said Brand wryly.

'Well, Matthew! He's not himself. I hadn't realized he'd crack up so badly. I'm sorry. I really must rush, so much to clear up.'

'What will you do? Now that the film's shut down.'

'Who knows?' Then she brightened up. 'But I've had a call from David Puttnam's secretary.'

'That sounds promising.'

'Well, you never know. It's all swings and roundabouts in this game.'

She turned on her heel, then paused and looked back. 'I'll keep in touch. I really will.'

The manager of the Mariahof was distinctly icy as he promised Brand he'd have his bill made up for him first thing in the morning. He'd never get a head porter as efficient as Fritz Sommer and for that he blamed this unwelcome guest.

'By the way, Herr Brand, there was a telephone message for you from England. An Inspector Waller? He asked you to return his call.'

Waller was tied up in a conference when Brand phoned but he broke off for a few moments while making it plain that Brand had been wasting his valuable time.

'I managed to get that information you wanted, although God knows why you want it. That girl—who was it?— Knödel something?'

'Elke Knödel.'

'She worked as nursemaid for a chap named Preissing in the German Embassy in London just before the war.'

'I told you that. But what happened to her?'

'Hang on. Let me finish. It seems she married an Englishman, settled in Peckham. He was called up for the army and killed in Tobruk.'

'And Elke?'

'Died in an air raid in 1941. Sort of ironic, don't you think?'

'You're right, Waller. It's sort of ironic.'

As he put down the phone, Brand began to laugh uncontrollably. For several minutes he couldn't stop. It was as if all the pent-up tension of the last few days was flooding out of him in that cleansing fit of laughter. Elke Knödel, that good little Nazi who had been responsible for destroying a family and several other lives fifty years later in doing her duty for the fatherland, had been killed by a German bomb dropped over London in 1941.

Oh Fritz, he thought, if only you'd known!

Then he pulled himself together, packed the bulk of his luggage for the morning and promised himself a final last look at Salzburg, smiling benignly in the late spring sunshine under the brooding presence of the Hohensalzburg Fortress.

Although its leading man had been cleared of any suspicion that he'd murdered his wife there was no reprieve for *The Sound of Murder*. The movie was shelved and the crew paid off. But the distribution company that put up the major finance collected on the insurance and salvaged some of the footage for use as background material in another movie set in Austria.

After riding high for a further six months Louis Wilder was ousted in a power struggle purge when the film division was taken over by an electronics corporation. He's now heavily into debt and cable Television.

From time to time Jake Schneider announces in the trade press that he is in the process of negotiating a multi-million dollar picture deal with Clint Eastwood, Robert Redford or Dustin Hoffman, which is news to Clint Eastwood, Robert Redford and Dustin Hoffman.

When Brand last heard from Debbie Price she'd finally landed a movie with David Puttnam and was disciplining the natives on location somewhere up the Amazon.

Matthew Armstrong didn't become a superstar. An attempt to resurrect *Braddock* on TV was a failure and his ratings plummeted. When Martin Elliott left him he took up with a younger man and began drinking excessively on set as well as off. He still appears on the stage and screen, playing interesting character roles that aren't too demanding. The critics tend to be kind. But his friends in the business say he's never been the same man since his wife died.